Autumn On Esereth

MOLLY MEYER-ALLYN

ISBN-13: 9780615777764
ISBN-10: 0615777767

Library of Congress Control Number: 2013904135
Molly Meyer-Allyn
Longmont, Colorado

www.autumnonesereth.com

CONTENTS

Acknowledgments

I would like to express my deepest gratitude to my husband for the constant, unending support during the process and evolution of this book. It was his patience, love, and humor that brought us to this place—together.

A thousand thanks to my sister, Ali, who just also happens to be the most amazing English teacher ever! She spent countless hours reviewing and providing her talented insight as this work evolved. She brings a great energy to everything that she does.

A big heartfelt thank you to Katrina for her help in bringing the true spirit of this book through in its cover and illustration designs. Her extraordinary talent and vision has truly enabled this book to ascend to the next level.

Here's to my sweet daughters. They help me, every day, to appreciate *just this moment.* They are the true teachers, not I. Thank you, girls, for helping me to look with new eyes upon this life!

Finally, I offer my love and thanks to my mom and dad, who have been my inspirational teachers throughout my life. They have always believed that I can accomplish whatever I set my mind to. They continue to help me learn, love, and look for opportunities to better understand myself and my role in this precious life.

PROLOGUE

OCTOBER 1992
EARTH

I love my family.
—Michael Allyn

The woman sat on the edge of the bed, openly sobbing as the man across from her packed a single black backpack. She leaned over to grab two new tissues from the bedside table and dabbed her mascara-stained tears.

"Please don't go," she pleaded.

The man paused from his task and walked over to her, kissing her on the lips and then hugging her tightly—hoping that somehow it would make things better for both of them.

"This breaks my heart. I love you—I love you so much," he said.

"Will you be able to come back?"

"I don't know."

"Will I ever see you again?"

"I don't know."

The admission of the unknown sent the woman further into the depths of despair. "She won't understand this."

He held her shoulders and looked into her eyes. "She cannot know why I left or where I'm from. You must promise me, Clara."

She nodded in reluctant agreement. She would do whatever he asked.

There was a knock at the bedroom door. A small set of brown eyes peeked around the corner.

"Daddy...come take me to bed!"

"My sweet Sara—yes, I'm coming."

CHAPTER 1

ESERETH

OCTOBER 2012
LOCATION UNKNOWN

*The direction of our lives is a path willed by the
energy we transfer to one another. In the midst of
what can sometimes seem like so much chaos,
to be sure, there is an intense purpose.*

Sara's consciousness came back not all at once, but
in stages. Each one was more progressive than the
one before it.

Emotions were the first to revive, in her case, one
emotion: *fear.* The trepidation was so overwhelming
and singly focused that it immediately fueled the next
phase: her body's response. She stood up, feet moving before her eyes were even fully open. It was an
almost violent transition from her previous sleep like
state to the new defensive and alert one. The adrenaline was pumping, and her breathing was raspy and

forced. The final stage invoked her senses. She was processing her surroundings now, although still in a heightened survival state. She saw that she was in an open pasture, alone, with the blackness of a massive forest looming just several feet from her. It was dusk, and only subtle hues and shadows from a fading light remained. She shook her head in almost stupefied denial.

Nothing was familiar.

"Where am I?" she asked herself.

Sara looked down at the small, worn, leather-bound book that was still gripped tightly in her hand. The book felt oddly more like an extension of her own self rather than a separate entity. Her mind flashed through recent events. She had just moments before been in her bedroom...hadn't she? She'd touched that book that was now so lifelessly still in her hand. It was after that simple touch that she had seen a brilliant flash of light and felt an excruciating pain through her entire body...and then...ended up right here.

Sara somehow managed to pull herself out of the paralyzing, mind-numbing fear that was gripping her mind and body. She forced herself to move. She took a deep breath and then willed one foot in front of the other. The direction didn't seem to matter, but she knew intuitively that if she stayed in this same spot, she would perish. She did not look back as she entered the thick canopy of the forest ahead of her.

It was a dense, unyielding forest that did not want to be traversed. As she pushed forward, she was walking blindly without the benefit of light and felt the branches scraping her, almost maliciously trying to hold her back. It was exhausting.

The sound of a large bird's wail overhead stopped her in her tracks. She attempted to still her ragged breathing, but her body resisted vehemently, insisting on the additional air.

Suddenly, there was a rustling of leaves and then the sound of a nearby fallen branch cracking.

She was not alone.

She instinctively turned toward the sounds and saw a very large human form bearing down in her direction. Before she could suck in the breath to scream, she felt a sharp and deliberate blow to her head.

And with that, her night and her vision faded into a black oblivion.

CHAPTER 2

EARTH

OCTOBER 17, 2012—ONE DAY EARLIER

There is harmony in autumn, and a lustre in its sky,
Which through the summer is not heard or seen,
As if it could not be, as if it had not been!
—Percy Bysshe Shelley

The small German town of Wald was gently nestled near the Black Forest. It was a quaint and friendly place with an Old World feel. Its location was just ten minutes from her grandmother's home. Sara had been staying there since her mother's passing just three weeks earlier.

Sara parked her small dark-blue Peugeot down a vacant alley several blocks from the town's outdoor marketplace. She was on a mission this morning to buy dinner for her and her grandmother. It was busy this time of day, and it had been extremely difficult to accomplish the basic task of finding a parking spot.

She stepped out of her car after fifteen minutes of circling the area, feeling disappointed with her lack of accomplishment.

She reached the entrance to the main thoroughfare of the market several minutes later. Sara let herself be taken into the current created by the people strolling along. She shook her head in amazement as she walked.

If the vast selection of fruits and vegetables, meats, fresh breads, and cheeses wasn't enough, the broad variety of crafts, books, clothing, and flowers would make up for it. She very much wished that there were more places like this available in the States.

She slowly drifted from covered stand to covered stand, looking at the wares and watching the people all around her. On her right, there was a man wearing a white hat and apron selling fresh meats. A customer talked to him while he worked to finish the order. He expertly wrapped two thick, raw steaks in white butcher paper then tied them with a neat twine bow. He had a small smile on his face as he listened to the customer speak. It was genuine, and it made her smile a little, too. On her left, she noted a stand with a display of fresh fruits. They were arranged, literally, in the form of a rainbow with the appropriate colors—apples, oranges, lemons, limes, blueberries, and even purple grapes. It was almost too beautiful to eat.

As she meandered through the shops, she could not stop her thoughts from briefly drifting toward her mother. She and Sara had been to this market more times than she could count over the years. It had always been such a treat as a child to be able to go with her and be a part of the expedition.

Sara sighed; her mother's death had been so sudden. She'd gotten the message from her grandmother that her mother was very ill and had immediately flown from her home in New York City to Wald. It was impossible to describe how she had felt seeing the barely recognizable, frail, and withered-away woman. Sara had sat by her bedside, grabbed her mother's hand, and wept. The vulnerability of life had come into full view. It would only be a few more hours until the end.

Her mother's last words were uttered in a ragged whisper to Sara. "I love you...and tell your father I love him, too." Her mother's mention of her father had further deepened the sadness of that moment.

Lost in her thoughts, she had hardly noticed that she'd moved away from most of the stands with actual edibles. She started to turn around in an effort to correct the overshoot but then noticed a kiosk just off the main way that had several chest-high bins full of old, worn books. There seemed to be no organization, and most of the books were just piled haphazardly on top of one another. Some had the covers half torn off, some looked dusty and dingy, and others, while fully intact, looked as if they'd been read a million times.

She saw no one manning the booth initially, but unexpectedly she caught a glimpse of the top of a head of curly blonde hair peeking above the stand counter. Then up came a pair of brown eyes and the face of a no-more-than-nine-or-ten-year-old girl. The girl moved from the stand to a red plastic chair next to the booth. Once she was seated, her legs were too short to reach the ground, and as a result they swayed just slightly back and forth in midair. The girl grabbed a book lying in the pile to her right and opened it. She hummed softly as she leafed through handfuls of its pages.

Sara was inexplicably drawn to this girl. Before she knew what was happening, she was standing less than two feet away from her and staring quite embarrassingly. Sensing Sara's proximity, the child looked up from her book, and they locked eyes. The girl's small, oval face seemed to speak of both wisdom and innocence.

They both stood in silence, observing each other for what seemed like an eternity but in reality was likely no more than a few seconds. The whole situation unnerved Sara, and because of this she suddenly had an impulse to hurry and move on, which she promptly started to act upon.

But unexpectedly girl stopped her. "Wait," she said, "I have something for you."

Still sitting in her seat, she reached over and pulled out another book from the pile next to her. This book was much smaller than the one she'd held. She gestured for Sara to take the book from her.

Sara obliged by taking it, and she immediately studied it with fascination. This volume almost looked like a cross between a book and a box. It was only about an inch thick and no more than five inches on its longest side. It had a dark-brown leather face with gold-colored scrolling around all the edges. It looked very old. The book was held shut with a thick leather-looking strip. It all seemed as if it was representing something—but what? A large keyhole was located precisely in the middle of the book face. The strip would not give way so that she could open it. The key was missing, and the book was locked.

It reminded her of the diaries she used to keep as a child. Only she had the key to her deepest thoughts and dreams. There were someone else's secrets in this book.

Sara shook her head and said to the little girl, "I'm sorry, but I cannot take this." She tried to hand it back.

The girl responded, "It is a gift—for you." The look in her beautiful eyes was so intense that she only had to say one more word. "Please."

And for reasons that she could not explain, Sara slid the book into her jacket pocket. The girl, seemingly done with their interaction, had gone back to reading her own book.

Sara turned and walked away from the booth and back onto the main street of the busy market.

෬

About thirty minutes later, Sara exited the market. She didn't think she could have bought one more thing and actually managed to lug it the distance back to her car. One of the good and bad things about these open markets was that you were limited by the amount that you could carry. There were no oversize shopping carts to be rolled out to your car. No, she had to walk four blocks with the two overfilled cloth bags that she had brought with her. Her arms started to ache severely from the strain of it, and this pain encouraged her to pick up the pace.

She was almost to the alleyway where she had left her car. The bags partially obscured the view of her feet, and because of this, as she transitioned from the sidewalk onto the road, stepping over the curb, she miscalculated and stumbled, twisting her ankle and very narrowly missing a nasty fall. She now had a nice sting in her ankle but was able to quickly regain her footing. It took several seconds of mental cursing before she was ready to begin to fully walk again.

Unfortunately, she'd been so focused on the annoyance of her ankle that she hadn't immediately noticed the muffled sounds of shoes on the pavement behind her. It wasn't until a car siren in the distance sounded that she turned her head around to look behind her and noticed two well-muscled men—both wearing black and walking in her direction.

She'd been taught to always be aware of her surroundings and to never put herself in a situation where she couldn't call for help. It struck her that not only might there be something wrong with this situation, but she was in a place where it would be difficult to call for help. That realization caused her heart to start beating rapidly. She forced herself to turn around once more in the hopes that she was overreacting, even a little delusional, but she saw that the men were looking directly at her as lions might stalk their prey. She heard them stepping in unison, with their pace now quickening. She picked up her own pace with the hope that she would reach her car before they reached her. It was her only escape. Even though her walk was now a jog, she kept mentally reassuring herself that no one would have the audacity or stupidity to mug a woman in broad daylight near a busy market with hundreds of people—right? She attempted, awkwardly, to hold both bags in one arm using her thigh as a prop so that she could get her key fob out of her front pocket. She felt a surge of frustration. All of this was taking too long.

Just as she had successfully secured her key fob, she was abruptly whipped around and grabbed painfully by the shoulders. The severity of that act caused her to drop all belongings including both grocery bags, spilling the contents onto the concrete. It was as she had feared; this was really happening. One of the men in black had ahold of her now and was staring harshly at her no more than just a few inches from her face.

"Should I scream?" she thought.

He seemed to have heard her thoughts because for no apparent reason he slapped her, hard, in the face. She was fighting a mixture of tears, outrage, and fear. Her face was flush, and the situation was getting more out of hand by the second.

"What do you want?" she cried. Now tears were starting to flow of their own accord, and this frustrated her even more.

The man who had her in his grip responded severely, "You are coming with us."

"Are you kidding me?" The response came out in an almost-hysterical laugh.

The other man said tersely to his partner, "Just grab her and let's go. We've got to get back. He's waiting for us." She'd read in several books how people rarely lived once kidnappers had taken them to the next location, and she had no intention of heading to the next place. The shock from the last several minutes started to fade, and her wits were slowly returning.

In that instant, she decided to stomp, hard, on the foot of the man who had ahold of her.

It worked…sort of.

It hadn't really hurt him as she'd hoped, but he was surprised long enough for her to start a short sprint. She had gotten a whole ten feet from him before the other man tackled her to the ground. He had grasped her hair and was getting ready to drag her to her feet. She could feel blood from her now scraped knees starting to bleed through her jeans.

Her despair at that moment was all encompassing. She'd just thrown away her one chance for escape.

It was at that moment of resignation and fear that she heard a low rustling behind her and then a loud thud. Suddenly, she was released.

She turned around. Someone had just come to her rescue and knocked down the man holding her! Her attacker now lay on the ground moaning in pain. And as relieved as she was for the help, she wasn't going to stick around to say thank you.

She started to run. Behind her, the man who had saved her suddenly let out a grunt of pain. She involuntarily turned back to see that her other assailant had struck her rescuer in the face. He was now the newly redirected target. She struggled intensely between her own fear and her guilt over the possibility that this man, who had just obviously tried to help her, would be hurt, or worse, killed.

She made her decision.

She turned, took a deep breath, and started to run back down the alley toward the men. She did the first thing that came to her mind. She yelled, very loudly, "I'm over here!"

Her attacker jerked in surprise and stopped to look in her direction for the briefest of moments. This was just enough of a distraction to allow her rescuer the opportunity to deliver a very hard-fisted punch to the man's face.

Both attackers, now battered, decided in that moment on retreat. They headed down the alley back toward the main street and disappeared within seconds. Her rescuer did not chase them.

Everything around her had gotten very quiet. She couldn't believe what had just happened, or that it had ended this way. Her defender steadily walked toward her, and as he did she started backing up. A feeling of trepidation was quickly returning.

"You have nothing to fear from me," he said.

She stopped her retreat and looked at him, really looked at him, for the first time. Staring at her was a set of stunning blue eyes. The bluest and most entrancing eyes she had ever seen.

"Are you all right?" he asked.

"I...I'm sorry. Yes."

That seemed to be sufficient, and he started to turn away.

"Wait!" she said with some small amount of desperation.

He stopped and turned toward her for a moment. They looked at each other, both feeling the intensity of the moment. They were connecting. Something was happening.

He swung around and ran in the opposite direction down the alleyway into the darkness.

After he had disappeared into the shadows, Sara turned around and started walking briskly toward her car. Once there she attempted to retrieve the key fob that lay partially obscured underneath the vehicle. It was the frustration of this simple task that melted her remaining composure. Against her own harsh admonishment, she started to sob uncontrollably.

But despite the emotional breakdown, she somehow managed to get into her car, lock the door, and pick up her cell phone to call the police.

 ❧

She and her grandmother ate leftovers for dinner that night, as the bags of groceries she had bought were likely still lying on the sidewalk in the alleyway. The only thing that had managed to stay with her was the book she had gotten from the little girl. It had remained inconspicuously tucked into her jacket pocket.

The police had been unhelpful. She felt certain that they would provide no real assistance in ever finding the men who had attacked her. After they had left, she had shown the book to her grandmother and told her the full day's events. Her grandmother hadn't said much. Instead she'd only looked intently at the book and nodded very slowly.

As Sara walked up the staircase to her room after dinner, book in hand, she thought about how much her grandmother's actions had perplexed her. It was definitely not the reaction she would have expected. It was almost as if she hadn't been surprised about the book or about the attack on her.

She flipped on the lights to the room she was staying in and walked over to the small desk next to her bed. She laid the book down.

"What an insane day," she thought.

She felt horrible. In fact, she felt in general as though life were throwing her one thing after the next that she didn't fully understand.

കൃ

Later that night Sara awoke in a sweat and breathing heavily—again. She looked over at her nightstand, the red numbers on the alarm clock feeling obnoxiously bright. It was three in the morning.

It had been almost twenty years since the night-mares had started. Twenty years since her father had left her and her mother. She'd been only eight at the time, but some days it felt as though it had happened only yesterday.

Some said he had abandoned them, but Sara knew deep in her heart that her father would never have done that; at least not willingly, anyway. Something horrible had happened, and she had no proof except for the nightmares that had followed her through childhood and continued, now, into adulthood. At times she'd felt as if she couldn't stand any of it any-more. Her dream always started the same way: She was running and out of breath. It was dark all around her, and that darkness was stifling. She was so scared. She didn't even know what she was running from, just that she was very frightened. It was in that moment, when she felt that she could bear no more of it, that her father would always appear. His strong hand was outstretched, beckoning her to come to him. But she never reached him. The dream would end, and she'd rouse in a cold sweat, her breathing ragged. Always in that moment of awakening, she'd be forced to relive the loss of her father. It was so real and so painful.

She lay back down and closed her eyes, desperately hoping for a more peaceful sleep.

∽

The next morning she was up early. It was crisp and cold out. The sun was now over the horizon, causing the leaves to glisten, almost proudly, in their newly turned coats of color. The days were winding down earlier, but the mornings, like this one, were brilliant and clear, and she loved them. Autumn was a time of change. It was a time of transition.

As she finished up her walk, meandering slowly down the wooded path toward her grandmother's estate, she tried desperately to think only about the harmony of this moment—only the trees around her, only the sight of her breath in the cool, brisk air, and only the dusty path ahead of her. She loved this place with its charm and its simple days. It was always a place that could calm her mind and make her feel whole again. Her grandmother, Lillian, on her mother's side, had inherited the German estate from her father and his father before him. It was the history of this place, her history, that made it so special.

She believed that there were these moments, these glimpses in which one could see purpose in life. However, just as quickly as those instants came, they vanished, and she was unmercifully thrown back into the flailing of everyday life left with only the intense need to try to find another moment like it. But after the first glimpse, she knew it was there, and she would strive to once again know it—to feel it.

She couldn't stop the insistent wandering of thoughts. There would be no peace—at least not today. She gave up trying to fight it and allowed her mind to drift into the abyss. This time the abyss took the form of her recent attack.

"What if they come after me again—or my grandmother?" she thought. "And who is the man who saved me?"

Despite his help, her sense of security and safety felt severely compromised. She wasn't even sure she wanted to go anywhere alone, at least not for a while. She just couldn't understand what they would have wanted from her.

She had already had to live most of her life as a nomad; she did not want—no, she refused—to let her last safe place be ruined by these unknown faces. She sighed, remembering how often she and her mother had moved when she was a child. It had started right after her father's disappearance. First London, then Paris, after that it was New York...The list went on. She had always thought it was her mother's way of dealing, or not dealing, with the abandonment, but in the later years of her youth she'd felt there was something more. As if they were running from something or someone. It was the same urge she was feeling right now.

Her thoughts reluctantly drifted back to reality as the forest path ended and her grandmother's house came into view. It sat nestled in a small clearing with the forest on all sides. Her grandmother was now her last living relative. She'd always managed to be there when Sara needed her most, and now was no different.

Sara was close enough to the house that she could see her grandmother sitting in the wooden bench swing on their covered front porch. She was entertaining a ritual of serious proportions, the soft, dark brown fleece blanket that Sara had gotten her recently for her birthday on her lap, an oversized yellow coffee mug in one hand and a book in the other. At that moment, as if feeling Sara's thoughts upon her, she looked up to see Sara approaching the house. A smile as bright as the sun formed on her face. Sara waved and then hurried into a slow jog up the narrow gravel drive to meet her.

"How was your walk?" her grandmother asked.

"Very beautiful," Sara said, her tone not as convincing as she would have liked.

Her grandmother gave her a look of understanding and replied, "Please come sit with me."

Sara nodded, walked up the stone steps of the porch, and sat down next to her.

She and her grandmother did not talk, but instead listened to the breeze, the birds, and the creak of the old bench swing. All in all very healing songs.

An hour later, Sara slowly stopped the swing, moved the blanket that they shared off her lap, and stood up.

Sara said, "I could sit here all day, but I should probably go upstairs to get cleaned up and changed."

Her grandmother nodded in response. Sara leaned over and hugged her grandmother.

As Sara headed from the front porch into the foyer, she stopped for a moment to look up at the stained-glass directly above her head. As a child she used to stand in this entryway and look up at the sky-light-like ceiling. She'd look so long that the back of her neck would ache from the strain of it. With its multitude of colors and designs, it had effortless grandeur. They most definitely didn't make them like this anymore. The white crown molding that bordered the ceiling was over two centuries old and still pristine. As she stepped over the threshold from the foyer, she took in a deep breath and thought, "There it was…just a moment."

She continued into the house through the main entryway and headed up the stairway to her room. She turned left down the hallway at the top of the stairs and stopped in front of her bedroom door. As she turned the doorknob, she swore she heard voices. She stilled her hand so that she could listen further—yes, something was still there. Against her better judgment, she ventured to finish turning the knob and cracked open her door. A low-pitched sound was emanating distinctly from her room. She looked around in an attempt to find its origin. It didn't take long, because the source of the sound was also the location of an iridescent green glow. It was the book she'd been given by that little girl at the market.

The hair on her arms began to stand up, and goose bumps formed. Her body was obviously giving her a message, and it was a message that she decidedly chose to ignore. The glow around the book was now intensifying with every passing second. In an almost trance-like state, she slowly walked through the door and over to the book.

It was whispering to her, *"Transitio in lucem. Salvum planetarum."*

She bent over the book, which was still sitting squarely on her writing desk, until her nose was just inches from the shining entity.

Then her hand, almost of its own accord, moved toward the book. It was outstretched with the need to physically connect.

And in that moment, with only one simple touch, there was a brilliant flash of light and a pain like nothing she'd ever felt.

Her life was about to be changed forever, and that flash was to be the last thing that Sara would remember on Earth.

CHAPTER 3

ESCAPE AND REUNION

ESERETH
PRESENT DAY

It is a wise father that knows his own child.
—William Shakespeare

Sara awoke to the smell of acrid smoke. It was thick and uncomfortable, and she felt as though it were strangling her. But that unpleasant sensation was nothing compared to the throbbing pain in her head. Without opening her eyes, she slowly raised her left hand to the source of the pain near her temple, immediately feeling a warm, sticky fluid that could only be blood. Unfortunately, before she could further process that particular injury, the movement of her arm uncovered another, likely more serious, affliction. There was a sharp pain in her forearm.

"Please don't let it be broken," she thought. She risked opening one eye to look at her arm. "OK," she thought, "nothing obvious, like bone sticking out!"

She turned her head just a bit and surveyed her surroundings. She remembered now the recent sequence of events—awakening on the ground in the woods, and then the blow to her head by an unknown assailant. She connected the events further; he must have brought her here.

She saw that she was in a very tiny, cramped room, lying in a small, lumpy bed that was barely the length of her body. Her boots, if stretched forward just another inch, could touch the footboard of the bed. Just beyond her feet, she saw the fiery source of the smoke that was filling her lungs. There was a small, gray stone fireplace about four feet in front of the bed on the back wall of the room. It was dirty and had obviously had seen years of constant use, as there was significant staining on the stone and surrounding hearth. Most of the smoke seemed to be entering the room instead of going out the chimney. Her eyes began to water as if to further reinforce the visual observation.

Suddenly, she heard muffled men's voices. There was more than one of them, she noted mentally.

The sounds were coming closer now and becoming clearer. It sounded as if they were arguing. As quick as lightning, she shut her eyes again, afraid they might see her in her wakeful state. She ventured to open her ears further, hopeful that she might get an inkling of what they wanted.

The sounds were growing even louder now. "Oh no," she thought, "they're coming in here!"

The voices were now just outside the room where Sara was being held. They were close enough now that she could understand some of what they were saying.

"When is Vasin expecting her?" one voice said gruffly, sounding slightly annoyed.

"I say we kill her and get it over with," another retorted.

"No, you can't do that. He wants her alive for now."

The words from her unknown aggressors shocked her. Sara couldn't believe this was actually happening to her. All of this was supposed to happen to unknown faces that she might read about in the newspaper or hear about on TV. It all led to one conclusion. She had to get out of here, and it was up to her.

Craning her head backward and opening her eyes to look at the wall that the headboard of the bed rested against, she could see that there was a small window located about six feet from the floor—just a few feet from the top of the headboard. That window was her obvious, and likely only, escape route. And she even managed to convince herself that she might actually be able to reach it and squeeze through to escape.

She slowly sat up, and in doing so a wave of nausea washed over her.

She closed her eyes, breathed deeply, and thought, "One step at a time. Do not vomit."

That moment of stillness seemed to be enough. She felt as though she could move now. And likely not a moment too soon. She stood up on the bed, all the while nursing her arm, and managed to step from the mattress to the top of the headboard of the bed. With one foot on the headboard and her good arm and fingers digging into the windowsill above, she was able to hoist both feet fully onto the headboard so that she was positioned with her arms lying on the windowsill. From there she used her right arm to push open the window and in doing so felt the brisk cold air hit her face. That encouraged her.

"Keep going," she thought. "You're almost there, and you *can* do this."

She stood on her tiptoes and started to wiggle through the opening. It almost would have looked like an army crawl, but she was only using her arms, her legs now almost horizontal with the window. She was able to get the majority of her body through the opening. Next was a headfirst somersault, albeit a poor one, out of the window and down. Unfortunately, with only one good arm, she was not able to completely protect her potentially broken arm from the impact with the ground. The pain from that gymnastic feat was enough to draw tears and an involuntary grunt of pain. She lay on her back, taking deep breaths to steady herself.

In her horizontal position, instead of seeing trees, as she would have expected, she saw a clear, starry sky. The house where she had been held was in the middle of a small clearing with the forest beginning about fifty feet away on every side of it. Out of the corner of her eye, she caught the moonlight. Still lying on her back, she turned her head toward it, but where she should have seen one moon, she saw, instead, *two.*

She shook her head, closed her eyes, and opened them again. Still two. She was certain that the crack to her head had caused her vision to blur, because what she thought she was seeing right now was impossible.

Her attention was suddenly brought back to a more pressing predicament. Her escape hadn't been a moment too soon, and she wasn't out of danger yet. The men must have noticed her absence. There were four of them, each filing out of the house single file and then breaking off into different directions. She had no time to lose. It was nothing short of pure agony to pull herself up into a standing position and begin a run toward the camouflage of the forest. As she transitioned from the threshold of the clearing into the forest, she turned her head back toward the house to see how far ahead she was of her pursuers. One man was heading in her direction but was over ten feet away, and she didn't think he could actually see her. Hopefully she still had an advantage, and with that, a chance. She faced forward and picked up her pace.

Suddenly, and seemingly out of nowhere, a dark shape appeared directly in front of her. She did not have time to alter her course or to stop and so ran smack into it. She would have fallen backward directly onto her bottom if this form had not grabbed her by the arms. She looked up, expecting to see that one of her captors had found her, but instead she saw a very familiar face gazing down upon her. It took her a moment to focus in the dark, but then suddenly she felt a huge wave of emotion. Deep, old feelings from her youth washed over her…because it was the face of her *father* that looked down upon her, just like in her dreams. And with that, she promptly fainted.

ᢙ

Almost two hours later, the ache in her arm brought her back to a state of consciousness and immediately to her first question.

Had her father really been there? Or more likely, had she been imagining things in response to the stress of her current situation?

That last thought was put on hold as the feeling of nausea began to creep up into her throat again.

"Damn my head," she thought. She was starting to feel certain that she had a concussion, because of the nausea and the blackouts. She started to sit up, but with her eyes still closed for fear that if she opened them, she would surely vomit. Before she was in full sitting position, she felt a firm hand rest upon her shoulder, applying just enough pressure to push her back down.

As this was happening, she heard a masculine voice gently say, "Please, rest."

She lay back, allowing this shadow of a person to control her for the moment. She felt that she was lying on something hard and cold. It was probably the ground. That fact combined with the gentle voice made her feel certain that her initial captors hadn't found her and brought her back to that small house in the clearing. She also could feel the comfort of what must have been a nearby fire to warm her chilled bones. These changes in her situation were enough to encourage her to open her eyes, and as her vision came into focus, she saw a familiar set of blue eyes staring at her—the blue eyes that had saved her once before from attackers.

"You. It's you from the market."

He nodded in affirmation.

"Where's my father?"

He did not answer this question. This made her feel insecure. She hadn't imagined her father, had she?

In place of a verbal response, he opened a small metallic box the size of a loaf of bread. It looked very similar to a medical kit, and that initial assessment was further strengthened by its contents—gauze, three liquid-filled dark green vials, and one clear, empty vial.

The man proceeded to mix several drops of the contents from each of the three dark green bottles together into the single clear vial. After doing that, the vial took on an iridescent green glow. At first it reminded her of some sort of science experiment, but then the glow became so bright that it almost blinded her. Then, without warning, it started to vibrate.

She involuntarily jerked backward at this.

"Don't worry...It won't hurt. This should have you feeling better in no time." He poured the glowing liquid onto a square piece of gauze-like material then transferred it to the injured portion of her head. It went on cool, but then immediately started to heat up. The warmth only stayed a few minutes, then cooled again. In awe she found that not only had the pain gone away, but when she ran her fingers over where her wound should have been, she couldn't even feel a scar.

"How is that possible?" she asked out loud, more to herself than anyone else.

The man started through the same process again with the vials, presumably for her left forearm, but Sara didn't know that she quite trusted this *stuff,* whatever it was.

"Not yet," she told him simply. This was all too crazy—all too fantastic. She needed the pain in her arm at this point to remind herself that she was still alive and that some things were still as she would have expected.

He seemed to understand the deeper meaning of the request, and he replied, "Then I will tend to it later." He stood up and walked over to the other side of the camp.

Feeling a little better despite her arm, she took the opportunity to fully sit up and survey her surroundings. There were close to thirty men working all around her in the dark of the forest. They were all busy with some sort of task—tending to horses, setting up tents, cleaning gear. It felt very much like some sort of military encampment. Nothing could have looked this organized otherwise. As she looked past the men, she saw that beyond this small clearing, the forest was very dense all around them. It was in this moment that Sara began to really understand her quagmire. She had no idea where she was. Maybe she was in the forest near her home? She tried desperately to search for some logic but found none.

She surveyed the small group of men sitting on the other side of the large campfire. Her eyes darted from dark form to dark form. It was then that she saw him. The darkness of night and the shadows being cast by the nearby fire did not matter. She knew beyond a doubt that it was indeed her father. He *was* real. He was speaking to a man on his left, but then at that moment his eyes shifted and were suddenly upon on her. Seeing her awake, he held up a hand to the man, who followed his eyes and then nodded with an understanding look.

Her father walked over, kneeled down on the ground next to her, and then drew her to him and hugged her with an intensity that communicated all of the feelings of happiness and relief that they both were feeling.

She pulled away from him and said, "How is this possible?" She knew the answer. It wasn't.

Then he spoke. "I know you must have a lot of questions, and I will answer all of them, but for now you need to rest. Tomorrow we have a long day of traveling ahead of us."

Sara couldn't believe the familiarity in his voice. She immediately felt the warmth, wisdom, and safety of her childhood. It washed over her, providing both grace and clarity. He was still just as she had remembered him.

Suddenly, that moment made her feel as though something wasn't quite right—he should not still be *just* as she had remembered him. "He hasn't aged a day," she thought as she studied his features closer.

In fact, he looked just several years older than herself. She focused further, narrowing her eyes to try to disprove her initial observations. Unfortunately, her eyes did not provide the data she needed. She did not see the graying hair and age of someone who should have been her father. She did not see the distinctive wrinkles or the laugh lines of someone who should have been in his fifties.

Despite this surge of tenderness she felt, she forced herself to focus on the insanity of her current situation and the lack of answers she had.

What started out as her slow and calm reply turned into an all-encompassing ramble of needs. "I need to know now what is going on. I need to know why you left us all those years ago. I need to know where I am."

Her world had just been shifted upside down, and she needed to have some answers.

Her father sighed, then spoke. "You are no longer on your planet, Sara, you are no longer on Earth. You are on the planet named Esereth."

In turn, she gave him a blank stare.

He continued gently, "You have been through a huge ordeal, and you are most definitely in no shape to handle anything more tonight."

This statement seemed to shake her of her mental shock. She suddenly retorted, "Anything more? Yes, I *can* handle it!" raising her voice a little higher with each word. And as if to further emphasize that statement of fact she asked, "Why do you look so young? Why haven't you aged?"

"Sara, Esereth and Earth do not process time in the same way. Every ten years on Earth is equivalent to one year on Esereth."

And with that bomb now dropped, in a very fatherly voice he continued, "Sara, please get some rest and we'll talk more tomorrow."

෭ᘓ

Between her sore arm, the cold hard ground, and the shocking answers to her questions, she slept horribly. It also didn't help that they were up and moving just before dawn. She'd probably gotten no more than three or four hours of sleep.

They packed up camp quickly. Sara was given only a few minutes to smooth her rumpled clothing, splash some water on her face, and have a bit of bread. As she packed her few temporary belongings onto her horse, she noted the book that she still kept with her. It had been a quiet passenger since her arrival here.

She walked over toward her father. He was having a discussion with two other men. She desperately wanted to talk with him more, preferably before they left camp. Once on the move she doubted there would be many opportunities.

"Sara, good morning."

"Good morning, Father." She cut to the chase. "I wanted to see if we could talk."

"Sara, I'm sorry, we'll have to wait until this evening. There is too much to do before we leave camp, and if we don't begin our trek soon we won't make the distance required before dusk."

Sara was extremely disappointed. Waiting until this evening might as well have been forever. She needed answers now.

∞

They had been traveling for only a couple of hours, but she was already tired and sore. She'd not yet let the blue-eyed man tend to her arm, and so it burned horribly. It didn't help that it had been several years since she'd been on a horse, let alone on one for hours at a time. She knew that her thighs would ache and feel jelly-like by the end of today.

She had to find out more about her situation and where she was to go next, if she was going to keep her sanity. Her father's words from last night still echoed in her mind. "You are no longer on your planet." This was a man she had not known since she was a child. It was a man who was as much family as he was a stranger. She was even more bewildered by the term *your planet*. Was Earth not his, too? She was starting to give herself a headache.

She turned to her surroundings. Looking down at the thick layers of leaves on the forest floor as they rode, she noted that the foliage was shades of green, amber, and red. It was obviously autumn here, just as it was back on Earth. This planet was almost identical to Earth physically, at least as best she could tell. There seemed to be distinct cultural differences, which she had observed in the men she had met so far, but those were no more foreign than some of the different societies on Earth. And the ability to heal that they had, while miraculous, also did not directly indicate another planet. It had been the combination of two distinct opportunities of observation that had provided the substantive proof she needed to convert her into a believer that she had truly left her own planet. The first was the two moons overhead that she had observed the night of her capture. The additional orb was hard to argue against, and for now she was going to assume that what she had seen was not a figment of her imagination. The second indicator was not so far away as the moon. It was her father…and in particular his youth. Over twenty years had gone by since he had left her when she was eight years old. This living evidence was almost too much for her to process.

One thing was for certain: she must pay very close attention to everything around her. Something subtle might hold the truths she needed to understand this place and ultimately to get home.

All of the riders were at least six feet tall, broad shouldered, and very muscular. There were no women in the group save Sara. Their clothing was that of a medieval play. They were all dressed in tunics of red and black. They all had the expected amount of dirt and grunge accumulated from days of riding. These men had definitely been out for a period of time. Each man carried a sword and a shield. The metal of the sword was an iridescent magenta color. The shield was also magenta, but lusterless and matte in tone. This detail spoke perhaps of how the material was processed.

All of the men had been coolly polite to Sara last night and this morning. Their respect and aloofness seemed to stem from some unknown source. Obviously she did not belong here, but there was something else they seemed to know that she didn't. Determined to get more information than her father had been willing to give her last night, she gave her horse a nudge and moved up closer to the blue-eyed man who was riding on the horse just in front of her.

"Good morning," she said.

He turned and gave a small nod in response but said nothing.

She decided to continue, although she was a little nervous. "You know, I never got to thank you for what you did to help me...back on Earth."

"Of course," he replied. He gave her a long and intense stare. It was so deep that she blushed and looked down at the black mane of her horse.

He continued, "I'm Daric."

This was encouraging. "How is it that you were there to rescue me from those men that day?" Sara asked.

He perked up a little. That question seemed to be something he might be willing to discuss. "Your father sent me."

Sara nodded but still felt skeptical. Were there many people from Esereth on Earth? How did they travel back and forth?

"How do you do it then? I mean…travel?"

"It's through a bridge that Shalin created."

This wasn't making sense. "I don't understand."

"Well," he chuckled, "I'm not sure we understand completely either. What we do know is that the existence of Shalin somehow keeps the bridge in place. The first time you travel you need Shalin with you; it shows you how to access the bridge. After the first time, a person can find the entrance on their own."

She asked in response, "How are you able to find the bridge on your own? Where is it located?" She wondered if this was the way for her to return home.

"The gate isn't a place really; at least not in the physical world as we know it. It's a portal accessed through a perfect alignment with the present moment. It's most like what people on Earth might call *meditation*."

She nodded slowly. Things were getting more confusing by the moment. Another part of his explanation didn't make sense to her. "You keep mentioning this Shalin…what is that?"

He looked at her as if he was about to tell her something significant, but then he seemed to think better of it. "It's not my place to tell you about Shalin, Sara. You'll need to talk to your father."

Sara couldn't help but wonder what the connection was between Shalin and how she had gotten here.

Daric's voice took on a more serious tone. "There's a great war looming here, Sara. It would be the first ever in the history of Esereth unless we stop it...stop *him*." He leaned over from his horse to briefly touch her arm. It was a gesture of comfort, but she felt as if she had been shocked by his touch. "Your father will tell you what you need to know when it is time. We should keep moving."

He pushed his jet-black horse forward and left her behind him to process all that he had said.

They traveled until just before dusk, at least from what she could tell. It had become very overcast and looked as if some wet weather might be moving in. Along with the clouds forming, the temperature had dropped a good twenty degrees. And, as if it were some sort of weather vane to confirm this change, her arm and shoulder felt a newfound throbbing. She'd been relieved to see that they were stopping for the night. She was sorry now that she had not let Daric heal her arm. She was going to need every bit of her strength to make it through this ordeal.

She had assumed they'd be camping as they had done the night before, but to her surprise, out of nowhere a small village appeared. They'd been almost on top of it before she'd noticed the small thatched houses and mud huts. It was nestled carefully in the forest, hidden from everyone and everything. It looked to be inhabited by only about a hundred people, all of them living very simply. The feel of this world, more and more, was that of her own planet, just in another time. The men in the village were dressed in tunics and pants similar to the men traveling with her father. The women were in dresses that went down to their ankles. The clothes on everyone in the village were colored with the browns and greens of the forest. The people stood, briefly suspending their daily tasks, looking at the group as it rode through the main thoroughfare. Her father called a halt once they reached a cluster of several dwellings.

A man materialized from a hut directly in front of her father and his mare. He said, "Kalen, welcome. It is so good to see you and your men."

He was a very tall, older man. His presence was striking. If not for his freely flowing, snow-white hair, she would have thought him much younger. He looked serious and wise. He was wearing a simple brown tunic similar to the other village people, but she could discern that he was not the same.

In one fluid motion, her father dismounted the horse and grasped the man's hand in a familiar gesture. Kalen followed him into the nearby hut from which the man had just emerged.

Sara, no doubt, would have to find out who this man was, but first she needed desperately to get off this horse. It had been nearly five hours since their last break, and the thought of standing on solid ground was inviting, but it was also daunting. She wasn't sure she could actually make her legs work once her feet hit the ground. It had been years since she had ridden a horse, and at this moment she knew she was going to be horribly sore just from the riding itself. It had worked muscles she had not used in a very long time. As she started to pull her foot out of the stirrup, she felt a strong hand around her calf. It was Daric.

"You're tired, and your arm is not yet healed; let me help you down," he said.

He had surprised her, and had she been any less exhausted her pride might have argued with him, but not today. She offered him her hands, but he instead chose to grasp her around her waist; then he effortlessly lifted her down from the horse. This embarrassed her, as she was not expecting the intimacy. She awkwardly thanked him and turned quickly to walk away. She felt even sillier when she realized she didn't really even have any place to go. She stopped after a couple of steps and turned around, in doing so locking eyes with Daric. He had still been watching her. She could feel an energy, a connection, starting to grow with this man. It unnerved her.

She found an old stump near one of the huts and decided to sit. The villagers had made some initial offerings of bread, water, and blankets to Sara and the men. For the next hour she sat with a blanket on her lap, nibbled on a miniature baguette of bread, and watched from that location while men unloaded horses and gear. The village people jumped to help everyone settle in. It was nice to see that at least they seemed to be welcome here. The men and the villagers were speaking in a mix of English and a language she did not know. What really amazed her about supposedly being on another planet was that the people here, for the most part, seemed to speak English. The similarities between Earth and Esereth were, overall, extremely unsettling.

She saw Daric now walking toward her. He had changed clothes and was wearing a light blue tunic. He looked clean-shaven, much more relaxed, and very attractive. The pure strength of him was overwhelming. It made her think about how unattractive she must look. She'd not seen anything close to a bath or a mirror in what felt like a lifetime. She looked down, at that realization, not really wanting to meet his eyes.

What was wrong with her? She wasn't usually so caught up in such silliness.

He touched her hand, causing her eyes to lift, and said, "Come with me."

She silently followed him. He stopped just before the entrance of a small mud hut, turned, and said, "This is where you will spend the night."

He continued into the structure with Sara close behind him. It took a minute for her eyes to adjust, but when they did, she saw a small wooden table and two chairs, as well as an unlit fireplace. She was very aware of the fact that they were alone in this dwarf-like space. He must have felt it, too, as he took a deep breath then took two steps away from her and back toward the door.

He stood at the entrance for just a minute, contemplating, before he walked back toward her and said, "There are clean clothes and a basin to wash, but before that, I need to finish healing your arm and shoulder."

"Oh, OK," she said awkwardly.

She sat down at the table to let him tend to her arm. There was a small healing kit in an armoire next to the table. He laid out its contents, similar to what he'd used before, side by side on the table. Neither said a word while he worked. Sara kept her eyes focused on her arm for most of the time but would steal small glances when she thought Daric was not looking. When he was done, she was amazed at how well her arm felt.

"Thank you."

Daric stood up and said, "When you're ready, your father would like to see you."

He did not wait for her to reply, instead briskly walking through the exit of the hut. The wooden door clicked shut of its own accord behind him. On some level she was disappointed that he had left so abruptly, but she was also somewhat relieved. She needed some time to herself. As she looked down at her own muddy jeans and beige cotton long-sleeved button-down shirt, she realized how strange she must look to the people here. With a small surge of vanity, and despite exhaustion, she set out to look better than she felt.

Stepping out of the hut some thirty minutes later, she wore a dark green dress that Daric had left for her. Her hair was no longer in a ponytail but instead freely flowing down her back. She was not very happy with the clothing she'd been given to wear. The bodice was tight and low, and the waistline was high. The dress flowed down to her ankles. Her boots had been replaced with a pair of slipper-like shoes. The shoes, unexpectedly, were actually pretty practical. They were sturdy and very comfortable. She likened them to moccasins. And while it felt very good to be in clean clothes, she wasn't sure this particular outfit was going to last past morning. There was no way she was going to be able to ride in this. She decided then that she need to discuss with Daric the possibility of getting some more practical clothes, in particular, pants.

Since exiting her hut, she'd been looking for her father. As far as she could tell, he had not yet come out of the hut and was still talking with the white-haired man. She started in the direction of where she had seen him enter, and as she walked she could feel the stares of the men from her father's army. She felt more self-conscious than ever.

Sara took a long, deep breath, exhaled, and then knocked on the door where she believed her father to be. She stood waiting for a moment, wondering if she had been right, but just as she started to turn away she felt the door give way and saw a pair of dark eyes that belonged to one of the men looking at her. He motioned her inside the dark structure. She had to bend her head just slightly to make it through the entrance of the hut. Once in, though, she was surprised by the size of it. It was a good two to three times larger than the one she had been given. The only light came from a simple stone fireplace on the left side of the room. But she didn't need the light; she knew where her father was and gravitated toward him. She walked over to a small wooden table where her father and the white-haired man both sat. Her father pointed to an empty chair next to his and said, "Sara, please sit with us." She complied.

Her father then touched her hand and said, "We've been waiting for you; I want you to meet someone." He leaned over and put his other hand on the man's shoulder and said, "This is my old friend Aurek."

Sara sat there feeling out of place as this man looked at her with a keen curiosity. Aurek surprised her by saying, "Sara, I see that you are every bit of your father."

She blushed at this. Her whole life she'd been told that she favored her father. They both had thick, curly, dark brown hair and brown eyes. And in personality there were similarities, too. They both had an intensity and a charisma that drew people to them. It was hard to explain, but anyone who met them knew it was there immediately.

Aurek said, "We were just discussing the latest whereabouts of Vasin's patrols."

Vasin—she knew that name. It had been spoken by the men who had kidnapped her and held her captive.

Her father seemed to recognize this and said, "Sara, it's time you understood a little more about this place and what is happening here."

Sara turned herself and the chair she sat in just slightly away from the table so that she could better feel the warmth coming from the fireplace. As she waited for him to begin, she felt herself leaning involuntarily toward the fire. It was as if somehow the warmth would help strengthen her against what she was about to learn.

Her father spoke in a low whisper. "Sara, I was born on this planet—the planet Esereth."

Sara, shocked, jerked her head away from the fire to look at her father and responded, "What? No." It was so fundamental. What he was saying could not be true.

Her father took her hand and squeezed it. He kept ahold of her while he continued, "There is more. You need to understand the larger relationship between our worlds. Esereth exists in a different universe from Earth, but our universes are 'twins.' They are identical in form and born of the same cosmic mother, so to speak. Because of this relationship, our two worlds, and more importantly their respective life forces are also physically and cosmically connected."

Aurek added, "It is due to this connection that we believe our evolutions and destinies are also intertwined. "

These words caused her to look at Aurek and say, "Wait, what do you mean?"

Aurek paused for a moment and then said, "If life on one planet were to be completely destroyed, then life on the other planet would inevitably be destroyed as well."

Sara shook her head with understanding, but now there were new questions. "How is that even possible...to destroy *all* life?" she asked.

"Besides through action of the cosmos, there is only one other way. It is through the actions of humanity."

This caused Sara suck in her breath sharply. "Surely humans do not have that power? To destroy all life on the planet!"

"Human beings have more power than they know."

Kalen said, "This universal and worldly connection has a central guardian—Shalin. We are all bound by Shalin. It is an ancient book that chronicles the connection that both Earth and Esereth share with one another. But it is more than that. Not only does Shalin hold the past, present, and future of our two worlds, but the book is a physical, cosmic bridge between the two planets and our universes."

She thought back to her earlier conversation with Daric and his mention of Shalin...and she thought about *her* book. Her suspicions were slowly being confirmed. The same book she carried now. The same book that seemed to warm the oversize pocket of her dress at this very moment as if knowing that it was being talked about. The same book that had been key in transporting her here was also Shalin.

Kalen, as if hearing her thoughts, said, "Shalin's existence is the reason the people of Esereth are able to travel to Earth and back."

Aurek added, "But no one born on Earth can travel to Esereth. It is a limitation of the bridge." He paused, then continued, "That was...until you, Sara."

Sara's eyes were big as saucers.

Her father asked Sara, "Do you remember anything about how you got here?"

She responded shaking her head. "It's fuzzy. I was in my bedroom…then there was a bright light…pain. And when I woke up, I was here."

"Nothing else you can remember?" he asked.

"No." For reasons Sara was not quite certain about, she had omitted mention of the book.

Aurek continued, "The force of the book is older than life itself. It was here before us and will be here after us. The book is an unexplained enchantment that has brought both science and the metaphysical together.

Kalen said, "Sara, the man we spoke of, Vasin, is willing to sacrifice the very foundations of this world to try to sever the connection between Earth and Esereth. He believes that he is saving our planet, but I am afraid that his actions will ultimately cause the very thing that he is trying to stop from happening— the destruction of the people of Esereth."

"I know who you're talking about," Sara said quietly. "He was the one who was trying to kidnap me."

Her father nodded his head solemnly in agreement. "Yes, and he is the same man who ordered your attack on Earth."

Her father stood up from the table and took a step forward, so that he was standing next to Sara. Then in a voice that chilled her to her very soul, he said, "Sara, this battle we are in was brought on by a man who, if not stopped, will end up destroying both of our worlds. I don't know why you were brought here, but be sure it is for a very important purpose."

Later that night she lay on the small cot inside her sleeping quarters trying, unsuccessfully, to quiet her mind for sleep. The information her father and Aurek had given her was almost more than she could process. She was not important. How could any of this possibly be related to her? She couldn't believe that, at least not yet, anyway.

She thought about why she had chosen not to mention or show the book to her father or Aurek. It had not been a conscious decision at the time, but now, as she thought about it more, she felt as though it was because a small part of her did not quite trust anyone on this world, not even her father. And until she better understood her full purpose here, she was resolved to keep the book to herself.

CHAPTER 4

KIDNAPPED

To be taken from one's loved ones
must be the most horrible thing.

Just before dawn the next morning, they left the
small village that had been their safe haven. As
they rode, Sara and her horse were separated from
the other men by a thick, white blanket of dense fog.
She could just barely see the tail of the horse walking
in front of her. Not only did the fog blind her, but the
sounds around her were also muffled. Initially, it created a surprisingly serene isolation, but as time went
on, the separation damned her to her own disturbing
thoughts.

She was annoyed as she thought about the argu-
ment with Daric this morning. When he'd brought
in that long, heavy dress to her, it had almost been
laughable. Apparently, she had jumped about two
hundred years into the past with respect to wom-
en's rights in clothing. It seemed so silly now and

completely unimportant, but it was about the only thing she had, or should have had, control over recently. He had insisted that she not be allowed to wear the tunic and pants that the men were wearing. She had been firm and insistent in her request, as her own clothes were ruined from the mud and mess of the last few days, and the dress she had been given was completely unsuitable for the wild terrain they'd be traversing.

After all that arguing, she had compromised but at least not completely given in. Sara had worn men's pants and modified her dress by cutting it midknee. She'd kept the slippers, the new pair that still continued to be practical, and they had proved to be high enough around her ankles to keep from chafing her while she rode her horse. When Daric saw her, he gave her a frustrated look but said nothing more on the topic. She silently thanked him for that.

Daric had told her that morning that they were headed to a city called Antek. Different tribes were gathering there to prepare for the possibility of an all-out battle with Vasin.

Just a few weeks earlier, Vasin's troops had approached several of the nearby villages asking for their loyalty. All resisted, and as a result they were attacked and many of their homes destroyed. It was a devastating message. This violence was exacerbated by the fact that these people had lived a thousand years in relative peace and harmony. Vasin was not leaving the people a choice, and for that reason many tribes were fighting against him. That level of fundamentalism and intolerance was too much for these people. The fear was prompting people to start to take sides. The metaphorical walls were going up. This was quickly becoming a fight to preserve their very way life. Kalen had insisted the only way to truly end this was to meet Vasin head on. In order to do that they would need many men, supplies, and most important, time.

They stopped midmorning for a short break to water the horses, stretch, and refresh. Sara slowly eased off her horse onto the ground, careful not to further worsen her already sore person, and then untied a small, dark brown leather canteen from the saddle of her horse.

Out of the corner of her eye, she saw movement within the forest. A reddish-brown animal the size of a small dog with large ears and a bushy tail with a white tip emerged. Following just behind it was a smaller version of itself. It was a baby. They both stopped for a moment and stared at Sara.

"That's like your fox...on Earth," pointed out Daric.

She jerked in surprise at his voice. This also caused the animals to disappear back into the camouflage of the forest.

"Yes, that's what I was thinking," she responded.

"From what we've been able to observe, many of the animals on Earth are also on Esereth. It's difficult to tell if there are any that are truly unique to one planet or another."

It had also occurred to her that many of the plants seemed to be the same as on Earth, too. She responded, "We haven't even discovered all of the species on Earth. We'll likely never know, will we?"

He nodded in agreement.

"Why is it, do you think, that Earth and Esereth ended up so similar?" she asked. "How is that even probable?"

"It's been said that they are each in the same location relative to their own universe."

She gave him a questioning look.

He continued, "Earth and Esereth were born into similar cosmic climates. And those climates are driven by their relative location—their address—within their universe. On a cosmic scale, this means that the flavor of physics in each location is also the same—which in our case means the recipe for life."

"Wait, are you saying that basic physics can change depending on location?"

"Yes. Even in your own universe, depending on your location, the laws of physics may vary just a bit."

"I thought that the laws of physics were the one absolute in the universe that *didn't* change."

He nodded, understanding her challenge. "This compatibility and this match in the laws that we have is also at least in part the reason we believe we can travel between universes. It's why the bridge is able to work."

Suddenly she heard her father's voice call the group. "Back on the horses!"

That ended the conversation. Daric headed back to his horse, and she took a quick sip of water before mounting. It was a lot to think about.

They emerged from the forest a few hours later and saw the sun small and high above the horizon. Ahead of them, several hundred feet away, two great stone structures materialized. One looked like a pyramid, and the other, right next to it, was the opposite, like an upside-down pyramid. The upside-down version's fundamental shape and placement seemed to defy the laws of physics. Despite definitely being man-made they both somehow managed to be more extensions of the land around them than artificially placed. Sara and the men were still a good ten to fifteen miles away from Antek, and it seemed odd that they would be located there with nothing else around them.

Her father rode up next to Sara. This was the first time they'd been near each other all day. He'd been in the front, leading the entourage, with Sara riding near the back next to Daric.

He said to her, seemingly knowing where her thoughts were focused, "This is a death marker. We perform a ceremony here for people who have passed away. It's similar to a funeral for people on Earth. The marker itself is meant to represent the two separate events that occur with death. The first is the transition of the human physical form back to Esereth, and the second is the journey of the life force—or what some on Earth have called the soul."

"Where does the life force go?" she asked.

"It travels back to the source of all life."

◌

A few hours later, and now just a few miles outside of the city walls of Antek, they brought their horses to a stop for the night. The horses, the men, and Sara were exhausted, and all agreed that it would be best to make camp for the night, then travel the remainder of the distance to the city first thing in the morning. The clearing they chose was just barely big enough to fit all of the men, the gear, and the horses. It most definitely made for cozy camping, with the trees encircling them like a fenced perimeter. Sara wasn't sure if it made her feel safe or trapped. She had unloaded the bags from her horse and set up a small bed of blankets next to a lone, large, thick tree just on the edge of the encampment. It probably would have been safer closer to the center, as they were somewhat exposed in the clearing, but she needed a place where she could have some space to herself. She noted that the tree next to her rudimentary bed looked just like the spruce trees near her grandmother's home.

Once her bedding was prepared, she looked for her father.

She walked the circumference of the camp, twice, but was unable to find him. She knew that several of the men had gone out hunting small game for dinner. It was very likely that he was with them. She finally gave up looking for him and instead walked over and sat next to the bonfire that had been started by the men.

Soon after she was settled, Daric walked up and gestured to the space next to her. "May I?" he asked.

She nodded but felt hesitant.

They both sat looking at the fire at first, saying nothing.

Daric finally broke the silence. "How are you doing...with all of *this*?"

"All things considered, I think I'm doing pretty well," she responded.

He nodded. "You know...your father and I were pretty shocked when we saw you for the first time the other night."

"You and me both!" she blurted out.

He laughed. "I suppose even more so for you."

She felt as though the metaphorical ice was officially broken. "It's hard to believe this is happening to me."

"It's a lot to take in," he said, agreeing with her.

She felt as if she needed to talk about more normal things. "Daric, do you have a family here on Esereth? Wife? Children?"

"No wife or children." He glanced at her with something more than the statement implied. The subtle implication of his facial expression made her face feel warm with embarrassment.

He continued, "My parents and two sisters live in a village about one week's journey from here. I, unfortunately, do not get to visit them all that often."

She felt as if she needed to tell him something about herself. "I don't have any brothers or sisters."

"I know," he said simply.

How much did he already know about her? How much did any of them know about her?

"Tell me more about your life on Earth," he continued.

"I live in a place called New York City. Have you ever been there during your travels to Earth?"

"No, I have not."

"It's an amazing city. It's a diverse place built upon many different layers of culture and history. There are many opportunities there."

"Opportunities for what?"

"Opportunities to advance your career, for one." She shifted in her seat and stretched her legs out in front of her so they were closer to the fire.

He lifted a brow with a questioning look and asked, "What is a *career*?"

She couldn't help but chuckle. "It's a job, but I guess you could say that it's more than just a job."

"And so what is your career?" he asked.

"I'm an architect. I help to design buildings." It was time for trivia. "Did you know that there are well over a million buildings in New York City?"

He looked visibly impressed. He asked, "How many people must live there to need that many buildings?"

"It's the largest city in our country. It has something like eight million people."

He shook his head in disbelief. "That's an astounding number of people in one place. On Esereth there are, at most, several thousand that have come together to live. Do you have problems trying to get that many people to live together? "

She continued, "Cities the size of New York do have many problems; they certainly see more crime and pollution, for instance." She suddenly had a question for Daric. "How many people are on Esereth?"

"I don't know. I don't believe we've ever counted."

"We are so different," she responded.

"We are more alike than you think, Sara."

Discussing her thoughts with Daric that night was, for the first time in a long time, a comfort. Sara felt a little happier, and it seemed Daric did, too, despite the larger situation.

She watched him walk toward his small, makeshift camp to settle in for the night and couldn't help but note his muscular shoulders and broad gait. He made her feel safe, which was a new emotion for her on this planet. She carried that feeling with her as she walked over to her own bed to lie down for some much-needed sleep.

ᕳᕲ

Deep in the night, Sara was jerked out of her slumber. She involuntarily lurched into a sitting position at the sounds of several men yelling and nearby horses rustling and snorting with apprehension. Still half asleep, her heart thumping loudly in her chest, she stood up, paying no attention to the scattered blankets around her but instead concentrating completely on what was ahead of her in the dark night so that she might find out what the commotion was about. She didn't know what, but she knew that something was very wrong.

Suddenly, two men emerged from the darkness not five feet from her. They were locked in a violent struggle, delivering hard and deliberate blows to each other. As they came closer, she could see that one man was from their camp; the other did not look familiar and wore a green tunic, unlike her father's men who were typically in red garb. Sara's presence caused both men to pause for just an instant, and the man from her camp took advantage of the small distraction by grabbing the unknown man in a headlock and dragging him to the ground. They continued to wrestle, but before her father's man could get the assailant completely under control, the unknown man drew a large knife that had been hidden under his tunic and in one swift motion stabbed his opponent in the chest. The man from camp crumpled to the ground, and the other quickly got up and headed back into the darkness.

"Oh, God," Sara thought as that last violent act sank in. She was shaking now, and the feeling of security she had just barely begun to feel was now gone, replaced with raw fear. She backed away slowly from her current position and crouched next to a nearby bush. She could feel this fear gripping her, causing a paralysis that she knew could ultimately get her killed.

She took a couple of long deep breaths and told herself severely, "Relax—I *must* keep it together."

As if to prove that she could do this, she turned and crawled over toward the man who had just been stabbed, placing a hand on his wounded chest. She asked, "Can you hear me? I'm going to get help..."

Before she could finish her sentence, he started convulsing and coughing up blood. His body lurched forward with a force that was not his own, and he grabbed her arm and said, "Go...leave here."

She shook her head no and instead tried to stop the bleeding by applying pressure to his chest. The proximity caused her eyes to meet his, and to her disbelief she could actually see the hazy film of death starting to cloud his eyes. The sudden loneliness she felt in this realization was suffocating. Was this what it was going to feel like when she died? She could not, would not, face the raw finality of what was likely to become of this man. She needed to help him. She looked around, hoping to see someone who could provide assistance. Upon shifting her focus from her current situation, she could see that this attack was much bigger than just one man. She could not tell anymore who was part of her group and who her enemies were. The men were fighting openly now with an unknown number of assailants. Swords were flying. She could hear the cold, hard steel as the weapons met. The clash created a momentary high-pitched scream that was deafening.

Where was her father? Where was Daric?

As if hearing her, Daric appeared out of the cloudy abyss and dragged her to her feet, yelling, "We must get you out here!"

She was inclined not to argue and started toward the darkness with him. He brought her to a gathering of brush just inside the forest canvas.

"You must stay here. You'll be safe. I will come right back for you. I must find Kalen and get the horses."

"No," she said, "don't leave me here. We must get help together."

He held her shoulders, looked firmly into her eyes, and said, "You'll be safe, Sara, just *stay* here."

He ran back into the chaos of the night. She stood there stunned. Her father…She must do something to help him. She could not stay here. Despite what Daric had just told her, she moved away from her refuge amid the fighting and confusion to find her father. She had to.

She'd not gotten more than several feet from her haven when a fist smacked her hard in the face; then her scream was stifled by a hand on her mouth. She struggled, and as a result she felt a new tear in her previously injured arm, and this time was worse than the first. This pain caused her to involuntarily moan and abruptly stop the struggle.

The faceless man whispered, "Don't move." Dark, piercing eyes were looking down at her. She felt herself quickly lifted from the ground onto a horse. The man mounted the horse with her and roughly wrapped one hand around her waist.

"You try to escape, and I will kill you. Do you understand me?"

Sara stifled a sob and gave a curt nod.

With that, Sara and her captor took off into the night.

Only once they'd gotten several miles from camp and far away from her possible rescue did her captor let the horse's pace slow. His grip around her waist lightened a little, too. She took that opportunity to lift her head and attempt a deep breath. Her lungs expanded to take in the cold, thick air, but it did nothing for the raw fear she still felt.

Early morning now was upon them. It had not only brought with it the fear of the unknown but also a heavy layer of frost. There was a white icy coat weighing down the branches on the nearby trees. And if she hadn't been so involved with her momentary situation, she would have thought it very pretty. Instead she shivered. He must have noticed, as she immediately felt him drape a blanket over her shoulders. Her body betrayed her as she involuntarily leaned into the warmth of the blanket and the warmth of this man. She hated herself for that weakness.

They continued riding late into the day. It was almost dusk. In the past she had always gotten such comfort from the slow, lingering transition from day to night, the sun, shifting lazily toward the horizon, bringing with it shades of red, gold, purple, and green. She knew she would have no such consolation on this day. The foreign sun did not give her solace. And the night, the blackness, now threatened to wrap itself around this place—no, around her—with a suffocating stillness. She tried, unsuccessfully, to resist what seemed like an inevitable fate by desperately clinging to the final breath of bluish-purple light that was now just barely visible above shadowed treetops. It was no use. She was now truly alone. And that dark solitude left her unguarded and vulnerable.

Just after dusk, her captor reined in the horse and stopped near a nestling of trees off the wooded dirt path they had been traveling upon. He jumped off the horse and pulled the gear down. He only had a few blankets and some simple supplies. Once he had finished, he turned toward her and lifted her down from the horse. She winced at the new pain in her arm. He saw this and paused, just a moment, as her feet touched the ground. They were only a few inches away from each other. She had to look up at him. He stood at least a foot taller than her five feet six inches. He had an intensity about him that made her own breath catch. He said nothing but pulled out a slender brown bag. It had strips of material and some tiny brown bottles.

He turned and told her matter-of-factly, "Give me your arm."

He worked quickly, and she did not fight him. She knew what he was about to do. She needed all her strength, and so she let him work. His touch was light and expert. She watched him finish the last of the dressing and could already feel her arm healing. She couldn't help the amazement she felt at this medicinal technology. He took the remaining salve and brought it toward her face where he had hit her.

She instinctively flinched and turned away from him. He paused, but then continued forward, gently dabbing her bruised face.

"I'm sorry," he said simply.

She looked at him as he worked. He had medium-length, wavy, brownish-blond hair and brown eyes. He had not shaved in several days and so had the golden-colored beginnings of a beard starting to form.

"What is it that you want?" she blurted out.

He looked at her thoughtfully, then replied, "You will find out in time, Sara."

He'd said her name. "How do you know me?"

"We all know who you are," he replied simply.

She didn't get a chance to ask what that meant, as he turned abruptly away from her and walked away to tend to the rest of the gear.

He didn't seem to care that she was standing there, able to run off at any instant. She looked into the black forest around her. The stream of consciousness that was filling her mind was about nothing but escape—escape—escape. In the depths of her mind she was screaming those words with a desperation and an intensity that made her limbs itch to dash through the woods and to safety, but she did not. She did not make one move. She knew, on some level, that this was neither the time nor the place to try. And maybe that in itself was survival—or death.

His words now echoed in her mind. "You try to escape, and I will kill you." How could a man who had just tended to her wounds really mean to harm her?

He seemed not to notice her internal struggle. Sara watched him as he gathered the dead brush nearby and skillfully started a fledgling fire. He was strong and muscular. He looked to be about her age, maybe a few years older. A few minutes later, the fire had grown larger, but it continued to feed hungrily on the wood it was provided. He pulled food from his pack and placed it in a bowl over the open fire. After a few minutes she could smell it, a familiar smell, a lot like the beef stews her father used to make for her when she was little. Across from this man, Sara sat with her knees pulled up to her chest and her hands locked around her knees.

"What am I going to do?" she asked herself. This situation seemed much bigger than just one man. Which, truth be told, frightened her even more than her captor.

Somewhat suddenly, he got up and walked toward her. She instinctively scooted away from him.

"Here." He leaned over and handed her a tiny wooden bowl with the thick, dark-brown stew staring back at her.

She shook her head and said, "I don't want it." But she did want it. She hadn't eaten since the night before and was very hungry, but she would see herself starve before she'd let him see that weakness.

"You need to eat. We have a long trip ahead of us tomorrow." He sat the bowl down next to her on the ground and walked back toward the fire. Before he sat, though, he turned and said simply, "My name is Aron."

She involuntarily looked up at him, and her eyes locked with his. She did not want to know this man, let alone his name.

Sometime later she lay on her side curled up in a ball next to the tree, the food still sitting beside her untouched. She was trying to sleep, albeit unsuccessfully. Between her mind chattering on and the fact that she was chilled to the bone, she knew this was an impossibility.

"Why is life doing this to me? What purpose could all this serve?" She touched Shalin, still in her dress pocket. This book was somehow connected to all of it.

She'd always felt with an intense certainty that everything happened for a reason, but today, yesterday, and the day before? None of it seemed to make any sense, and the feeling of doubt that was starting to well up into a knot in her throat was so very difficult to swallow. The peace and confidence she'd always been able to extract from the truth of life were not here tonight. Tears started to form in her eyes, but she forcibly willed them away.

She was so into her thoughts that she did not hear him the first time he softly called to her, and so it startled her when she finally heard him, and his voice had raised to a harsh command. "Come here, Sara."

She uncurled herself and turned toward him but did not get up. She only stared dumbly at him as he stood just a few feet away from her.

"Come over here," he repeated with authority.

That tone scared her tremendously, and so she slowly and reluctantly got up and crossed over to him.

"Lie down on the blanket," he said.

After she did this, he lay down directly next to her, in the spooning fashion, and put his arm around her waist.

She balked at this. "No, I will not."

And as she struggled to get up, his grip around her waist tightened.

"It's OK...I'm not going to do anything more." He sighed, somewhat exasperated. "This is the only way I can make sure you don't run off short of tying you to that tree over there."

Sara had no choice. And as she lay there, she could feel his strong arms around her, his hard chest pressed against her back, and his warm breath on her neck. She shuddered at the surge of intimacy between them.

"Who is he?" she thought. "And how am I going to get out of this mess?"

∞

Meanwhile, he was struggling to maintain his own composure as this woman, his captive, was lying next to him. She really was beautiful. Her soft form fit well next to his. He'd been shocked when he had seen her for the first time in the midst of all the havoc from the attack on her father, Kalen, and their men. The entire attack had been for one purpose: to cause enough distraction for him to bring her back to the city of Valina. Her innocence in this mess was obvious. There was an immediate attraction, but he knew he could not be with this woman. She had a larger destiny. She was to be the savior of them all.

୬

Sara and Aron started again early the next morning. Aron had the horse loaded even before she awoke, and they ate a quick and silent breakfast of bread and water. They'd not spoken since their brief encounter just before bed the night before, and this was fine with Sara, as a growing dread was starting to weigh heavily upon her. She did not want to reach her destination.

They traveled another few hours before the horse broke through the dense forest and into an open expanse. Once clear of the trees, Aron slowed the horse from a trot to a walk. Sara's eyes had to adjust to the newfound light, as the forest had let little of it in during their journey. Very quickly the open field was forgotten. As her vision cleared and her eyes shifted up from the field ahead of her, she saw it…a massive fortress nestled into the jagged cliffs into the distance. Beyond the cliffs she could see the white tips of a snow-covered mountain range that went on as far as the eye could see in either direction. The contrast between the dark cliffs and the white of snow was as striking as it was daunting.

The stronghold had a light brown stone wall circling it. It was clearly impenetrable. And the road leading up to it, if it could even be called that, with its dusty, rocky pavement and its narrow path looked treacherous. She felt as though the world was against her at every step, even in getting to the stronghold of her captor.

There was no way an army or large group could make it up this route. Their horse was struggling with its two passengers and gear. It had taken them the better part of the day to reach the entrance to the city. She could now see the city wall in full view looming just ahead of them. And this thing, this massive stone monster, represented the sum of everything that had happened to her thus far. The full realization of this caused her to suddenly and unexpectedly begin to cry. The streak of emotion that filled her was as uncontrollable as her need to breathe, and as much as she tried now to suppress it, she could not. In the end she gave way to every last piece of it and let out, in the form of tears, a wave of pure, absolute emotion that had been building inside of her.

He pulled her closer to him and grabbed her small, frail hand. This surprised her, but she felt oddly comforted and did not pull away. They then rode silently hand in hand toward Sara's fate.

Near the entrance of the gate, the guards, in a seemingly familiar gesture, exchanged nods with Aron. He had only had to barely slow the pace of their horse as it moved through the main drawbridge-like gate.

They stopped just past the portcullis. Dismounting, Aron handed the reins to another guard who stood waiting nearby. He helped Sara to the ground swiftly and then firmly grabbed her upper arm, guiding her toward the center of the city and to the largest building inside the gates. She could tell it was large but couldn't see much for the first several minutes of their walk through the city.

To get to their destination, they had to walk through the main thoroughfare. They did this for the most part unnoticed by the people who lived inside the citadel, who all seemed oblivious to this man and this woman alongside him. These people were obviously going about their daily business just as Sara would have back on Earth. The average person paid very little attention to others in those cases. She looked around and took in the sights. Even more than ever, she felt as though she'd jumped back in time about four hundred years. Most of the people were in very simple garb and were getting from place to place on foot or on horseback. There were small markets selling food and clothing.

Ahead of them was a grand palace, decorated with ornate arches and spiral towers. There were several large sections to it, all connected to one major central structure. They were so close now that she had to crane her head almost straight up to see the top of the construction.

There were two large, intricately carved wooden doors at least two stories high. The carvings on the doors consisted of foreign patterns and symbols. Twenty statues, all of men, lined either side of the entrance on a ledge about fifty feet up. She felt them staring down at her as they crossed the threshold. As they approached, the two doors opened outward, seemingly under their own power, letting both Sara and Aron enter. The physical beauty of the doors and the castle was evident, but considering her situation she felt more like this place was just waiting to devour her whole. It was not a good feeling.

Inside the doors, the area opened into an expansive great hall. She saw that the walls were made of stone, and the arched ceiling was at least fifty feet high. Beautiful stained-glass windows were all around her. The glass started just a couple of feet above floor level on every wall and traveled like a rainbow up the wall, across the top of the ceiling, and down the other side. The huge breadth of the windows allowed softly filtered streams of light into the room. The back wall was not covered by windows but instead had several large, dark-red tapestries. They were even more beautiful than the scores of tapestries she'd seen during her time in Europe. They had intricately embroidered pictures and stories on them. At first glance the story lines looked to be unrelated from mural to mural, but as she stared closer, each tapestry seemed to be a part of a larger story. She flinched involuntarily when she saw the tapestry in the middle of the wall. It had a large picture of a book, but not just any book—it was her book. The same scrolling, the circles, and the keyhole. It had to be. It was Shalin.

Now in the dead center of the hall, she was met by a bulky guard dressed in an ornately decorated dark green uniform. The edges of the uniform were lined with a gold-colored cloth, and the combination was grand and intimidating. He had what looked to be a sword holstered at his side.

She turned toward Aron with a look of fear and vulnerability. "Where am I going?" She wasn't sure what she thought he was going to say or do, but she wanted, no, needed him to assure her that everything was going to be all right. He didn't respond to her question verbally, but the look in his eyes communicated remorse. Instead of feeling comforted by what he might tell her, it had the opposite effect. It made her feel even more afraid. The guard moved forward and grabbed her arm, pulling her forward and ushering her farther into the main hall.

Once to the far end of the main hall, the guard released her and stepped back. Her eyes were drawn up to the ceiling toward the light coming from the windows.

She involuntarily jumped at the sound of a deep, booming voice that came from behind her. "Sara."

She turned around and saw the source of the sound. A man at least six feet tall, with broad shoulders and jet-black hair, stood just a few feet from her. He was dressed in a black tunic with gold lining similar to that of the guards. There was no doubt in her mind that he was a person of some significance. He looked powerful and scary. Actually, everything about him frightened her: his size, his voice. He started to walk toward her, hand outstretched, as if he were an old friend. She attempted to back away from him, only to be reminded of the fact that she had nowhere to go—nowhere to run.

She leaned forward a little and with a voice that sounded braver than she felt said, "What is it that you want?"

Ignoring her question he said, "My name is Vasin. You will be staying here with us for a time."

"You didn't answer my question," she retorted, feeling a burst of both courage and anger.

He looked at her for a moment as if deciding how to respond. He finally said, "You may either be treated as a guest or a prisoner. The choice is yours," he continued.

She lifted her chin forward and said, "I think the answer to that is obvious. I was kidnapped and brought here against my will. I am a prisoner in this place."

He sighed then responded to this by saying, "And that is your answer?"

She would not look at him now. She was done speaking.

He looked at her then said to the guard, "Take her."

The guard immediately grabbed her arm again and started pulling her back toward the entrance of this immense structure. She struggled against the man, but it only seemed to madden the guard and make her even more exhausted than she already was.

He took her down a narrow staircase near where they had entered the castle. She found herself in a small, dank cell made of stone. The guard unceremoniously dumped her to the ground before slamming the thick, heavy door behind him. She felt fear, disbelief, and annoyance. The combination created a livid woman.

What little light there was came from the sole window in the cell. That was if you could even call it a window. It was located just above eye level, probably only as big as her fist, and because of that fact let very little of anything in through its opening. It was almost dusk, and she knew before long it would become pitch black in this space. She stretched up onto her tiptoes to try to see through the small expanse. With some success she could see that the window was at street level, and she could see the feet of the many people who lived in this city walking past her. They shuffled along, all living their lives, none the wiser to her ordeal.

Gathering all she could for the moment from the window, she left it and walked over to a small cot that sat in the corner of the room. In observing it, she saw that there were relatively clean white sheets and a small pillow. She lay down on the makeshift bed and looked at the now-black ceiling about eight feet above. The exhaustion swiftly spread over her. As her mind started to fade into the oblivion of sleep, she vowed to herself that even at the risk of dying, she would free herself of this place. She had to.

❦

The next morning she awoke to a pair of small eyes staring directly at her, not two feet away from her bed. She yelped and jerked up into a sitting position. Her nerves were close to shot anyway, and this was the last thing she'd expected to wake up to this morning.

Those eyes belonged to a small boy, and he jumped back at her unexpected response and gave a shriek of his own. He looked no more than ten, with brown hair and green eyes. He wore a green tunic similar to the guards' garb. The scare caused him to back away toward the exit. It was a stare down, and while she could tell he was afraid, he didn't immediately request the guard, who she knew was just outside the door. He continued to look frightened, but he had managed, barely, to save the breakfast he carried on a tray from leaving his hands and hitting the floor.

She attempted, albeit poorly, to salvage this introduction. "Good morning."

That seemed to make things worse instead of better. He continued his escape by pushing his back up against the cell door.

"Wait," she said. "Don't go. Please...what is your name?"

He timidly responded, "Balu...I'm Balu."

She gave him a small smile, which seemed to thaw his fear a little. He stopped his retreat and instead just stood staring at her for close to a minute. She did not speak but sat quietly with him in the room, not wanting to spook him further.

He finally spoke. "Is it really you? Are you really the one who will save our planet?"

She looked at the little boy and wondered what people had been filling his head with. "Balu, I don't know what you're talking about. I've been kidnapped and am being held here against my will."

He shook his head and took a step forward, seeming to find some reservoir of courage. "Of course you're not. Vasin would never kidnap anyone. You are here so that you can end our conflict. So that we may have peace in our world."

She stared at him as though he had lost his mind.

He continued, more confidently now, "Vasin has spoken of you for a long time. He said that you would one day be sent to us—sent to save us."

The guard stepped into the cell and motioned that Balu should come out.

"I will come back to see you tomorrow," Balu said.

Sara nodded and then couldn't help herself—a small smile formed on her face as the little boy walked—no, almost skipped—out through the door of the cell. After the large guard slowly closed the massive portal to freedom, Sara's smile faded.

The rest of the day was a blur. She found herself sleeping a lot and secretly hoping that all of this might just be a bad dream. But it was not a dream; it was real. Later that night, she lay in bed wondering about her father.

"Is he OK? Is he thinking about me? Is he looking for me?"

She missed him so much. And she hated to admit it, but she'd thought a lot about Daric in the last few days, too. Her feelings for him had been growing swiftly since their first meeting back on Earth.

"Please let them be looking for me," she whispered to herself.

They were the only people on this world, literally, besides her captors, who knew she existed.

Almost in response to that thought, she felt a warmth against her side. She reached down into the pocket of her tunic and pulled out Shalin. She was surprised by the light green glow coming from the book. The glow increased for a few more moments, then dimmed until it finally looked like an ordinary book, and also as if it had told her what it needed to, but it hadn't. She'd never even seen inside the book. There was no key. She stroked her thumb over the keyhole. Sara turned the book on its side and spent the next several minutes trying to find a way to wedge her fingers under the strap to force it open. It would not budge.

"What's inside here?" she wondered. And what was her connection to it?

❦

Like a wounded animal, Daric paced the sparse tent he'd been staying in since they reached the city of Antek. He had been going mad since that horrible night. It had been his fault and his alone. He'd been charged to protect Sara, and he had failed. He had left her alone and helpless. Kalen had sent patrols out looking for Sara three nights in a row, but Daric knew that they would be unsuccessful. The attack had ended as abruptly as it had begun, and Daric knew the reason for that. They'd been after one thing that night—Sara—and they had gotten her. There could be only one man behind the attack.

He exited his own dwelling and walked toward Kalen's quarters. His mind raced toward the plan that they would execute to get her back. They would need to be swift and strong. The city of Valina, he knew, had to be where they'd taken her. It was well guarded, and they would have no choice but to raid the city to rescue her. The thought of her in that city with Vasin and his men for even one day made him crazy.

Daric opened the door and briskly marched into the shelter. "What's our plan? We need to begin the infiltration into Valina immediately."

Kalen was sitting in the center of the space at a small wooden table with his head bowed, reviewing the stack of papers that lay before him. He looked up at Daric with a knowing look.

Calmly he responded, "We need to wait, Daric. We cannot rescue her just yet."

Daric ran his hand through his hair in frustration and said, "What? Why not? We cannot leave her in Vasin's hands for even one more day. The man is crazy. We must get her out now!"

"There is no way that we can do a full-out attack on the city. It would be suicide for us and Sara. Valina is too heavily guarded, and there are too many innocents."

Daric responded, "What other choice do we have? We have to do something."

Kalen stood up, pushed the chair back from the table, and then walked up to Daric, putting a hand on his shoulder. "Daric, you must trust me."

Daric sighed heavily, knowing that he must do as he asked.

Kalen continued, "We will ensure that Vasin is brought to justice for what he has done to this world and to Sara. We *will* get her back."

Daric left the shelter still feeling very upset. He walked to the outskirts of the encampment and toward the forest. He saw some of the men practicing with swords, and so he walked over, picked up one of several swords propped up in a line against a wooden bench, and joined them. He needed release. The drills they ran focused on cutting, parrying, and drawing. The level of focus was key to any swordsman's success. As he set up to spar, his thoughts went again to Sara. He wasn't normally this emotional and crazed. Sara had done something to him. He'd known women in the past, but he'd always felt in control, and he'd never felt as though he *needed* them. In fact, it was usually the other way around. His sisters had chastised him over the years for breaking the hearts of women.

One of the men signaled for the match to begin. Daric's blade cut through the air, making immediate contact with the other man's blade. Both men were quick, with clean techniques, but it was quickly obvious that Daric was the more expert swordsman. The sparring was over within a couple of minutes, and the next man stepped into position to fight with Daric. And that's how it went. One by one he fought them with the hope that he could make these extreme feelings he felt for Sara soften. He was not successful in his quest.

Kalen sat in his hut and thought about his last two years here on Esereth. They had been fraught with fear, disagreements, and mistrust. And as much as his time on Earth had taught him about some of these same things, it had also instructed him about the amazing goodness of the people there. And certainly Sara, his daughter, had been his greatest teacher of all in that regard.

He'd been lucky enough to go back twice to Earth briefly to visit Sara and Clara. Aurek had cautioned him not to show himself to Sara because she would not understand why he'd left and why he had to leave again. The first time he traveled back to Earth she was at her high school graduation ceremony. She looked beautiful in her white gap and gown, and her smile shone brighter than anyone else in her class. He'd been able to visit Clara briefly on that trip as well. It had been both the happiest and most painful time of his life. They had both changed so much. For him it had been only a brief year; for them it had been a decade.

The second visit was just after Clara's death. He not found out she was sick until it was too late, and he'd not been able to make it back in time to see her before she passed away. He'd wanted to know that Sara would be OK. It was the only way that he, himself, could get through his own feelings of loss and emptiness. He'd been comforted to see that she was spending time with her grandmother, Lillian.

Now she was here, and he must make things right for her. The reason Sara was in such danger was because of him. The reason Vasin knew about Sara was because of him. The fact of her existence had come out during a recent attempt at negotiating with Vasin. He did not think Vasin would dare involve her, but as a precaution, he had sent Daric to watch over Sara on Earth. He never could have fathomed that Vasin would want to end her life when he learned of Sara's existence. Now, Kalen was the only one who could stop Vasin, and he would do it not only for his planet, but for Sara.

With these thoughts to guide him, Kalen stood up and walked out of his hut. He crossed over into Antek for a meeting with the tribes. The tribes' representatives had been gathering for weeks now, but it wasn't until this evening that everyone had arrived and was ready to discuss their future. There had not been so many of the tribes together at one time before. There had never been a reason.

Later that night, in a building deep within the city, Kalen and Aurek sat at the head of a long wooden table with the leaders.

Kalen stood up slowly from his seat and then said to them, "We have all come together here to discuss how we, as inhabitants of this planet, will stop Vasin from destroying our world." All of the men and women there agreed with nods and hushed murmurs.

Seeing the concurrence, Kalen continued, "Then let us begin."

CHAPTER 5

A CITIZEN OF VALINA

This city is what it is because our
citizens are what they are.
—Plato

O ne full week had gone by, and Sara was still sitting in her mental and physical prison. She knew she was working through the "stages of her captivity." She remembered reading something about denial and anger, but she wasn't completely sure how to classify the stage she was actually in. She only knew that she was an emotional wreck. She'd felt fear, sadness, disbelief, but most recently it had been frustration and anger that filled her thoughts.

"Where are Kalen and Daric? Why haven't they come for me?" she wondered with frustration. And who was Vasin to think he could do this to her?

To maintain her sanity, she forced herself to focus on parts of her life back on Earth. She had to be careful, though; not everything actually helped. If she let them, thoughts of her mother would break her down into tears. She still missed her very much.

Her friends and her job were relatively safe thoughts. Sara had started at her architectural firm just out of college. She had a great team and really loved the people she worked with. One of her closest friends and colleagues, Kyle, she'd known since college. He was always there for her and always willing to help with whatever she'd needed. They had done everything together for many years. She recalled a project in college where they were required to survey several of the architectural achievements in New York City. They'd settled on the Empire State Building, the Chrysler Building, and the Statue of Liberty. They'd spent weeks out at the locations and working to finish the project. They'd aced it, in no small part due to how well they worked together as a team. Not long before her trip to Germany to visit her mother, he'd told her that he wanted to be *more* than friends. At the time, it was a complication that Sara had not wanted to deal with. She didn't want to potentially ruin the safe and predictable relationship she had created, but compared to her current situation, she would have gladly chosen it.

She told herself that she would be freed of this place for the sole reason that she had another life that needed to be tended to. She did not belong here. Somehow just that fact had to be enough to make it happen.

The only bright point of each day was Balu. He dutifully came every day to bring her meals, and along with her food he gave her bits and pieces of very useful information. In the midst of all this madness, she felt as though she had started to make a friend. She learned that Aron was Vasin's second in command, and that Kalen, her father, was Valina's enemy. The people of Valina had been told that her father was trying to take control of their people. She could not believe that. She was sure that Vasin had somehow twisted the story to gain their loyalty and keep the fight going. This was the way of war, wasn't it? Twisting the truth until it met your needs and your desires? Us against them? How else was it possible to get people to believe that there was only one truth and that it happened to be their side that was fully and completely correct? It was difficult to know what was really the truth. There very likely was no such thing as real truth.

She remained very quiet during Balu's stories. She took in all the information and was waiting for the opportunity in which it would prove useful in her escape. He'd been timid at first, but she had gotten most of the information from him with little bribes. She would tell him something about her world, and he would return the favor. Yesterday, she had told him about automobiles. He'd stared at her in disbelief at first, but the more detail she had told him, the more she could see the shroud of skepticism lift and the excitement show through. By the end of the conversation, she'd hooked him. He couldn't get enough from her on the topic. She discussed the different shapes, sizes, and colors, how fast they could move, and how much they could carry. He'd been even more amazed when she told him there were over six hundred million motor vehicles on Earth. What struck her as oddest about her conversations with him was that he was completely comfortable with the existence of Earth. She supposed it was like knowing that the moon existed; although she herself had never been there, she comfortably knew that it existed nonetheless. She was happy to share all of this information because she had learned something very critical, and discouraging, as well…the layout of the city of Valina.

The city was a large semicircle embedded into the mountains, with only its city walls exposed to the outside world. It was, as she had suspected, completely impenetrable. There were guards posted all along the wall and at every exit. They were there every moment of the day. The majority of the homes were near the outer parts of the city, and the markets were near the center. The main palace was directly in the middle of the entire complex. It was also the oldest structure.

This information had kept her up all night thinking through any options for escape, but it was for naught. She had found nothing.

That next morning the proof of this planning was staring at her in the small, warped, round mirror on the wall next to the cot. The lighting was not great, but she could see well enough to note the dark circles that had started to form under her eyes. She shrugged at the notion that she should care what she looked like at this point and finished sweeping her hair into a ponytail at the nape of her neck. She then leaned over a bowl of warm, soapy water. She had been at least allowed to clean herself up in the mornings. Not a full-fledged bath, mind you, but a sponge cleaning was certainly better than nothing. She needed to get out of the prison; she just didn't know how.

Suddenly, as if in answer to her silent questions, Balu rushed into the cell. He was breathing hard, and for a moment Sara thought something was wrong. She relaxed just slightly when she saw the broad grin that broke on his face.

"Sara! Sara, I have some exciting news!" His laughter and enthusiasm were infectious.

"What is it?" she asked.

"We are beginning the preparations for Valina's three big festivals! There will be lots of music, drinks, and food, and everyone will be there, and..."

"Whoa, slow down, Balu. What are you celebrating?" she asked. She put her hand on his shoulder and chuckled despite herself.

"Our successful harvests, and the upcoming winter...and well, one another!"

"It sounds amazing," she said.

The grin on his face widened, and he said, "Oh, yes, this will be the best year yet!"

She spontaneously decided on her plan. "Balu, I would like very much to attend the celebration with you." He stopped, crinkled his little face as if thinking very hard, then said, "But how could you from here?"

"Well," she said, "I need to give Vasin a message. I want you to tell him that I am ready to be his guest. Can you tell him that?"

He nodded with such fervor, she couldn't help but be touched by his excitement.

"Yes, yes, Sara. I will tell him. I will tell him right away!"

He ran from the room, nearly tripping over the breakfast tray he had left on the floor earlier for her.

She had to think about her next step. She couldn't wait any longer for her father and Daric. She was going to escape by herself from the city.

Two days passed with no word from Vasin. To make things worse, Balu had not come back either. She was starting to feel the full effects of this place, and the weight of it was growing exponentially with each day. What would she do if he did not respond? What if she was really stuck in this jail with no other possibilities? She was becoming her own enemy.

On the afternoon of the third day of waiting, the guard opened the door and commanded, "Come with me."

She said nothing but stood up from where she sat on the cot and slowly followed him out of the stone cell up the stairs toward the main hall. She hadn't realized just how dark it had been in the cell until she was squinting madly at the light streaming through those stained-glass windows in the main hall. Because of this momentary blindness, she heard rather than saw Vasin.

"Sara, I'm glad to see that you've come to your senses."

She had to make every effort not to retort to this remark and instead forced a smile and said, "I have decided that I like being a guest better than a prisoner."

He laughed at this, a very deep, genuine laugh. "I thought maybe you might."

That laugh, it sounded somehow familiar. It was very unnerving.

In a low voice he said something to one of the men beside him. Then he said to Sara, "Follow Ifan to your room."

He pointed to an attractive young man with black hair standing in guard attire at the entrance of the hall. While still not certain what to expect, she sneaked a suspicious look at Vasin as she followed Ifan out of the hall. He was looking at her with a concentration that made her very nervous.

She walked up a staircase with a mahogany-like railing and wide white stone steps. The pathway curved in spiral form, with a long, narrow hallway meeting them at the top. As she walked down the hall, she observed that a combination of tapestries and landscape paintings covered the walls. They covered significant portions of the wall in between rooms. There was a new wooden door evenly spaced about every five feet. Ifan stopped in front of the last door before the corridor dead-ended. He opened it and extended his arm in a gesture for her to come inside.

It was a simple room, no bigger than any bedroom she'd had at home. A dark-brown, wooden four-poster bed sat in the left-hand corner of the room, neatly made with white sheets and a heavy beige comforter covering the bottom half of the bed. Two dark blue dresses lay on a knee-high chest just beyond the end of the bed. Large double glass doors lined the far wall of the room. One door was open, and she walked over to it. She crossed its threshold and stood on the small balcony on the other side. She could now see the palace's inner courtyard just below. She turned back toward the room, and on the wall opposite to the bed there was a large gray stone fireplace. She felt the wind pick up behind her. It whipped her hair forward and traveled through the doors and into the room. It caused one of the dresses on the edge of the chest to flutter slightly. The movement of air felt good on her skin; very few of the days were still mild, but today was an exception.

She was able to get cleaned up with a bowl of soapy water. And despite her muted protests to herself, she changed into one of the dresses laid out for her. Her clothes borrowed from Daric were a complete mess now, and she knew she had no choice.

As she turned away from the bed, she walked back out onto the balcony. Slowly stepping through the doors and out onto the terrace, she leaned over the side to better observe her surroundings. There was a considerable grouping of gardens in the courtyard. With autumn now here, there wasn't much actually growing, but she could only imagine how beautiful it was during the spring and summer months. A very large tree, perhaps an oak, stood in the center of the garden. With its wide trunk and far-reaching branches, it looked old and wise. The leaves were turning a striking mix of colors. It surprised her that so many leaves still remained on the tree. The forests around the city, she'd noted during her travels, had already lost the majority of their leaves. The sight was captivating, and for a moment she was lost in it. Lost until she caught a glimpse of the true cell holding her captive—she could see the city wall out of the corner of her eye in the distance. She had to figure out a way past the heavily guarded, looming wall, and the distraction of this upcoming festival was her chance to do this.

There was a sharp rap at her door, a short pause, and then the guard Ifan entered without waiting for her permission. She stepped back into the room to meet him.

"Vasin would like to see you in the library."

She was quickly learning to stifle all her outward emotions for the sake of her situation, but inwardly, she cursed him.

Sara followed Ifan toward the library. It was located on the opposite end of the palace, and it took them a few minutes of brisk walking to reach it. Once they arrived, she entered through two large, carved, almost black wooden doors. As she very slowly inched her way across the threshold, she was not able to stop herself from craning her neck upward to see what had to have been thousands of books around her and above her. They were all layered onto rich mahogany shelves that reached all the way up the thirty-foot ceiling. The crown molding was thick, with very detailed patterns, which added a majestic feel to the room. There was a small balcony that could be reached via the richly carved wooden spiral staircase. It reminded her of a tour she had once taken to the Biltmore Estate in North Carolina, except this was much bigger. And to top if off, the fireplace must have been at least eight feet high. It dwarfed her. The shadows from the flames leaped onto the books around her, giving everything an entrancing flicker.

She saw him. He had his back to her, looking out a large window on the far side of the room.

Vasin turned slowly as if sensing her presence. "Sara, hello. Have you settled in?"

She did not respond to this.

"I know what you must think of me for bringing you here, but it was the only way. I need to convince you of the truth."

"The truth? Why would I get the truth from you? You abducted and imprisoned me."

"You have now made the choice to be my guest, have you not?"

She was fuming now. How dare he twist this.

He continued, "I want to tell you about your father, about our disagreement, and most important, about the book."

In response to Vasin's mention of the book, Sara stopped and involuntarily touched her dress pocket where Shalin resided. The book was slowly becoming a part of her.

Fortunately, Vasin did not seem to notice this and continued on. "Sara, this fight between us has started because your father and I could not agree on the fate of the two worlds of Earth and Esereth. For two thousand years the people of Esereth have been the silent guardians of Earth. We have been able to do this, in part, because of the unique perspective that we possess—our different vantage point of Earth's time."

Her fingers involuntarily grabbed the folds of her dress in a fidgeting gesture as he spoke.

"We are also responsible for helping people on Earth to understand science and technology." He sighed shaking his head, "And in doing so, we unwittingly helped in forming our own demise. Sara, you see, it was my father who agreed to help plant the seeds of modern technology on Earth, just twenty-five years ago here and over two hundred and fifty on Earth."

He paused looking for a response from her.

She refused to give anything.

He gave her a nod, silently acknowledging her determination, and said, "It was the people of Esereth who enabled your people to emerge into the technological giants they are today, but it was a mistake. Your people took the basic information given to them and chose to take a different path from Esereth. You have used it to separate yourselves from the universe instead of becoming closer. You have used it to destroy instead of using it to heal. I have seen firsthand how you have decimated your wildlife and your forests and, worst of all, destroyed your own people through your wars. You have chosen to create great misery, not just for yourselves, but also for Earth. You have put into motion the global warming of the Earth. You have put the Earth out of balance. And for what? Power, corruption, and greed. People on Earth do not stop to ask if they should be doing something. You blindly move forward without thought about the greater conse-quences." He pulled together this information for her by adding, "Because the two planets are con-nected, life on Esereth will perish along with Earth if you do not change your ways…and we no longer believe that you will change."

Sara could not stifle her retort. She raised her voice much louder than she had meant to. "What is it that you think you're doing here with this war you're creating on Esereth?"

His eyebrows raised in surprise at her already complex understanding of the situation here. "Ah, Sara, this is different. This fight on Esereth is the first ever to take place on this planet. And if it is necessary to save Esereth…then so be it. The one war to end them all. The sacrifice of a few for the good of many. Sara, we have come to the conclusion that in order to have any hope of saving Esereth, the two planets must be separated. We cannot count on the people on Earth to change. So instead we must each be able to follow our own separate paths."

Sara felt stunned, not because she thought what he said sounded crazed, but because what he said made some sense…scarily so.

"This is all I will tell you tonight. You are not ready for the rest."

He turned and left her standing alone in the library. She was affected by his words, but she wasn't ready to believe that her father was wrong or that Vasin wasn't her enemy and the enemy of Earth.

Even though Vasin had told her to be down to the hall by dusk for dinner, she chose not to comply. She didn't care about what he'd do in response to her rebellion. She was in no mood for food and spent the remainder in the evening in her room sullen and scared. She fell asleep, still dressed, in her bed not long after dusk. She was so very tired.

⌒

She woke up the next day with a strong urge to get some fresh air. Her bedroom, even though the balcony doors were cracked open, felt stuffy and stifling. She sighed, knowing it was not the confines of her room but really this situation that was choking the life out of her. She needed desperately, even if just for a moment, to forget her situation. It was relief that she ached for.

Balu seemed to hear her silent plea. He came to visit her later that morning and suggested a walk through the nearby open market. She jumped at the offer. It was also a good opportunity to test the bounds of her so-called guest status.

As she left the palace and stepped out onto the streets of Valina, she shook her head in disbelief. It had been so easy, almost too easy. She had told her guard, Ifan, that she and Balu were heading into the city for the day. He had said, "Be back by dusk." Either they were overly confident that her escape skills were nonexistent, or this city really was impenetrable—or in her case, inescapable.

Shop after shop lined the narrow streets of Valina. These small, covered booths had many different items to offer, and it all felt very familiar.

She could see the beginnings of the festival preparation. They not only sold decorations for people's houses, in the form of small streamers and dried flowers, but they also sold "small gifts." Balu said that these, very similar to some of the customs on Earth, were meant to be shared with loved ones during the harvest and winter festivals. Amazingly, this simple act showed up over and over again often crossing cultural bounds, proof here, even on Esereth, that it was something more fundamental that likely defined us as human beings. Balu bounced giddily from shop to shop, explaining to her what the wares were and how they were used in Valina. His enthusiasm was contagious.

The food was the best. Sara couldn't possibly count all of the unique edibles on offer, all completely new to her. They went from stand to stand, sampling the many varieties. Vendors showcased the free selections on large white wooden trays. The food was cut into different shapes and arranged methodically.

Sara almost felt ashamed to ruin such carefully laid out artistry.

The people were friendly and genuinely interested in both Sara and Balu. They asked simple things. "How are you? How is your family? What would you like to try next?" All of this made her feel happy and allowed her to enjoy the moment.

As they sat on a bench eating small squares of recently acquired fresh bread samples, it made her think about the farming on this planet. She hadn't really seen anything of significance. At least not like the thousand-acre farms back on Earth.

"Balu, do the people here farm?"

His mouth was packed with bread, but he ventured to speak anyway. "Yesh." He paused to swallow. "For the most part, we only grow food near our homes. We grow just enough to eat and to trade."

This information spurred several other questions that had formed in her head.

"What about money? Do you ever use money to buy and sell items?"

"What is money?" he asked, confused.

She supposed that in itself was an answer. "Well, it mostly exists in the form of paper and metal pieces, and in recent history plastic credit cards and ones and zeros."

He gave her the funny look that her comment deserved. "I don't think we have any of that. We trade to get what we need."

"How about ownership? What do you own, Balu?"

He provided a blank stare.

She provided an example. "Do you own land?"

"How could we own it? It's a part of Esereth. It's a part of the universe."

His answer fed into a consistent philosophy that she saw here—that they were a part of versus separate from their surroundings. They were not, at least not until recently, as fundamentally driven by control or power over their surroundings. It was the control, ironically, that seemed to cause the separateness that she saw on Earth.

They stood up and continued down the row of kiosks. She saw one in particular that piqued her interest. It had more multipurpose items—camping gear, survival equipment—exactly what she needed during and after her escape from Valina.

But how could she acquire them? She had nothing to trade.

That wasn't true, she realized. Sara did have one thing. She looked down at the ring on the fourth finger of her right hand. The band was silver with a pearl the size of a small pea, simply set. Aside from the book, it was the last of what had come along with her from Earth. It was a ring that her mother had given her. It wasn't especially expensive, but it had special meaning to her, and now more than ever. She did not want to part with it but felt as if she had no choice. If it helped her to escape, then she must.

"Balu, I'd like to look at some of the things at that stand over there."

"Sure, Sara."

They walked over together to the red-haired lady in her forties who manned the booth.

"Hello," Sara said.

The woman nodded but did not respond.

"I would like to buy some of your things, but I don't have anything to trade except this ring."

The woman looked curiously at the ring out-stretched in Sara's hand. Her eyes got large. Sara wasn't sure if that was because she thought it special or complete junk.

The woman responded, "Yes, you trade the ring, and you can have everything on the counter."

"All of it?"

"Yes."

"Great!" yelled Balu, just as surprised as Sara.

Sara picked out a small duffel-like bag, rope, torches, healing salves and vials, something that looked like matches, and several types of ties and bungees. She felt a lump in her throat as she handed over the ring.

"Thank you," she told the woman and they walked away.

Balu suddenly stopped and said, "Wait, Sara, I have to do something quickly."

She watched him walk away into the crowd. With every day she was more thankful for this boy. He had become her only friend in this mess. She had learned a lot from him about the people in Valina. She had learned about their way of life and their day-to-day lives.

Balu returned within a minute or two, a smile on his face. She grabbed his hand, and they walked back toward the palace with their purchases.

Unexpectedly, they heard a commotion of horses and yelling. Balu immediately let go of her hand and started running toward the sound.

"Wait, Balu," she called after him. "You don't know what's going on! It might not be safe!"

But trying to yell on top of everyone else was useless in this large crowd of people, and so she took off after him instead. She looked around blindly for at least a minute before seeing his small brown head of hair among the gaggle of people gathered around something or someone. There was a young man lying under a large wagon. He was moaning and looked to be in a great amount of pain. Sara heard the man next to her say that the wagon had collapsed onto him while he had been working on its broken wheel. She started to move forward to see if she could help the man but was shoved backward by the people in front of her. They were making way for someone to come through. She could see just barely through the masses of people, but it was enough. She watched as a small, elderly woman hobbled her way toward the man. She was dressed very simply in a long blue dress, and her white hair was piled up on top of her head in a bun. She held a small black bag and looked very purposeful in her walk.

Balu had found his way back to Sara and whispered, out of breath, "That's the healer, Hecate."

Two men had managed to slide the injured man out from under the wagon. Sara watched as the woman expertly opened her black bag and brought out a small vial of light green liquid. The liquid started to glow as she covered the man's leg with it. Then the woman put her hands on his leg, and the glow got brighter. The woman seemed to be causing it. Suddenly there was a flash, and then the glow was gone. The people around looked on curiously but did nothing to make Sara think that this was anything new or different from what they had seen from this woman before. She watched as the man got up, shook the woman's hand, then started walking toward his wagon to inspect the wheel that had just crushed him minutes earlier.

This was similar to what Sara had experienced before with her head and her arm injuries, but that had not been of the same magnitude, nor had it been due to another person's seeming abilities. Hecate had instantaneously healed a broken bone! The crowd seemed to have seen what they came for, as they had started to scatter and get back to their daily routine.

Sara turned to Balu. "How is the healing done? There is nothing quite like this on Earth. That man can now walk as if the wagon had never crushed his leg."

"I don't really know," he responded honestly.

Sara realized at that moment that it must be somehow related to the connection these people had with their surroundings. She'd known most of her life that the technology of Earth had isolated its people. Humans purposely excluded and separated themselves from the rest of the world. She needed to meet this woman.

Even after the excitement of the morning, Balu announced, "I want you to meet my family."

This surprised her, and she paused before responding, "Yes, I'd like to meet your family, Balu."

She wasn't sure why she felt uncomfortable about the potential introduction. Maybe it was because of the circumstances surrounding this whole ordeal, but from Balu's perspective it was pretty simple, really. He liked her, and they were friends. He wanted her to meet his family.

They walked up to his family's hut together. At the entrance now, Balu turned and said to Sara, "Wait here for a moment." He entered the hut and shut the door behind him. She waited dutifully outside his home for close to five minutes. She began to wonder what was taking so long and hoped that nothing was wrong. Why hadn't he come back?

Finally, she pushed open the door to the hut and saw Balu was talking in a hushed tone to two smaller children, a girl and a boy, who were sitting on an oval brown rug on the floor near the fireplace. They were playing with a hand-carved wooden block set. The children looked like twins, and if she had to guess, were maybe four years of age.

The room was pretty dimly lit, which wasn't too different from many of the other houses in the city, but the mess she saw all around her was. The place looked as though it hadn't been cleaned in months. Garbage littered the floors, and dirty dishes were everywhere. The children also looked a little grungier than they probably should have been.

"Balu, who do we have here?" She tried to smile in a nonchalant way but felt a sensation of sadness, concern, and pity at the conditions they had been living in.

"Oh, this is my sister, Farica, and my brother, Taban."

The two looked up at her, smiled briefly, then went back to playing.

"Where are your parents, Balu?"

"My father is off on a mission for Vasin, and my mother has been gone since the twins were born."

"Balu, then who is looking after you all?"

"I am, at least until my father gets back."

"When will your father get back?"

"I'm sure very soon," he said confidently.

Sara, unfortunately, did not feel the same assurance that Balu did. These poor little ones had been alone for who knows how long. They seemed OK, but it was dangerous for them to be on their own like this.

She was determined to do what she could to help them.

"Balu, I want to help you get some things picked up and cleaned here, and then we'll talk with some of the people back at the palace about getting you, your brother, and your sister a place to stay there."

Balu started to disagree, but Sara cut him off, "Just until your father comes back."

He stopped the protest after that clarification. "OK, Sara."

Sara scrubbed dishes, wiped down furniture, and washed laundry. Balu, Farica, and Taban all had small jobs. They were excited to help, and she was surprised to say that it was actually real help versus trying to help. There were no modern advances such as vacuum cleaners or dishwashers to help in the tasks, so it took them awhile longer. Two hours later the small space was immaculate, and as a bonus Farica and Taban were also bathed and scrubbed clean.

She told them after they were done, "Let's head to the palace—*all* of us."

᠙

Upon returning to the palace from their trip out into the city, she asked one of the guards if they could keep the three children at the palace until their father returned. He looked unsure, at first, of quite what to do, but in the end he told her that he would discuss it with Vasin. That was a start.

Balu said his good-byes to Sara. He had decided to take his little brother and sister to the courtyard garden.

Sara started to head toward her bedroom but then saw another guard coming from the opposite side of the hall toward her. "Uh oh," she thought, "This probably isn't good."

He stopped a few feet from her and said, "Vasin would like to see you."

She followed the man back toward the library where they had spoken just the day before. As she reentered the space, she saw Vasin sitting a green oversize chair that looked very similar to her La-Z-Boy back home. He was reading one of the thousands of available books.

He looked up at her then put his book down on the nearby table sitting next to the chair. "How was your trip to the market?"

She asked, a little surprised that he would know that information, "How did you know that's where I went?"

He responded with no trace of sarcasm, "I know where all my guests spend their time." He luckily did not give her enough time to respond to that comment. "Sara, you are here to help us."

"I cannot help you."

"You're wrong. You're the key to separating our two worlds. You are the daughter of both Esereth and Earth. You are the daughter of our universes."

The blood from her face began to drain. "What is it exactly that you want from me?"

He continued, "You and Shalin are the only energies that link our two worlds, and through your *death*... and the destruction of Shalin...our fates can also be unlinked. Don't you see, Sara? You are our savior."

These last words pushed Sara over the edge. She had to get out. In shock, she started to back away from Vasin toward the door exit of the library. He had just blatantly spoken of her death. Any hope that he could be reasoned with was now gone. And what he foretold could not be true. He was manipulating her. He was twisting truths and telling lies.

Vasin continued on, "And it is once we find Shalin that you can complete your destiny to save us all."

She ran from the library as quickly as her feet would let her. A few minutes later, breathing hard, she found herself in front of the great tree in the courtyard garden. Tears were running down her cheeks. She pulled out Shalin from her pocket and looked at it. She did not want to die. She wasn't ready yet.

Time might not have healed all of Sara's recent mental wounds, but a night to deal with her situation gave her a surge of resolve and motivation to take charge of her predicament, and to do it before Vasin did. There was no way she was going to stay here. The only thing she seemed to have going for her at the moment was that he did not know the location of Shalin. That fact seemed to be the single thing that was keeping her alive. If he found the book, then she really was dead.

∾

The first of the larger autumn festivals that Balu had spoken of was this evening. Sara wasn't quite sure what to expect, but she knew that everyone in the castle had been working on the preparations, cooking, cleaning, building; it was nonstop. The excitement of the people was everywhere.

Sara was excited, too, but for a different reason: she was getting a bath, her first since ending up on this planet. The level of grunge and dirt that had built up felt like an impenetrable wall that mere water and soap did not have a chance of infiltrating, but she must still try. She'd been left a new dress and a bathrobe on the bed in her room. There were several baths in centralized locations throughout the city. Balu called them *balneum*. There was one balneum just outside of the palace. That morning as she walked toward it, she felt a little like she was going to the neighborhood swimming pool for a summer swim—except for certain subtle facts, like the fact that she could see her breath as she walked and that she was living in a medieval village.

Balu had told her that the baths, along with all of the potable water in Valina, were supplied by a nearby lake. He said that the water, using gravity alone, was transported underground into the city through an aqueduct-like construction.

She walked into the enclosed structure where she was told that the baths were supposed to be located. The warm, balmy air that immediately hit her confirmed a correct destination. She was standing in some sort of lobby where a man had been waiting for her.

"Come with me," he directed.

He led her to the stall where she would bathe. It was semiprivate with walls on either side, but open on top. There was another door on the opposite wall.

He pointed to it. "That is where you will exit when you are done."

"Thank you," she responded.

He left her to her task.

There was a ledge about a foot wide that spanned the circumference of the oval washroom. The bath itself was much like her bathtub at home. There was a spigot that stuck out from the wall. She pulled the lever next to it, and hot water quickly filled the space. Once it was filled, she stepped down into the bath and sat on a submerged stone bench—words could not describe how wonderful it felt. She was reminded of how much more appreciative human beings were when they had go without something for a period of time.

She scrubbed until her skin was blotchy and a little raw and then soaked for a ridiculous amount of time before reluctantly getting out and putting on her robe. She grabbed her dress, which was folded on the far ledge, and exited, entering a larger room with a series of medieval, if there was such a thing, wooden lockers. There were a good thirty or forty people, male and female, in this space, all dressing. She felt a little self-conscious, but she seemed to be the only one. She quickly dressed, gathered up her remaining items, and headed back to the castle. She felt like a new woman.

An hour later she stood in in front of the oval wall mirror next to the fireplace in her room, brushing her freely flowing thick brown hair in a repetitive motion. It was also an unconscious motion, as her mind was not on her hair but on her plan of escape. She was determined to use this night as an opportunity to survey her prison and come up with a way to leave this place. She knew it was dangerous, but based on Vasin's plans for her she could do no worse than try. If these celebrations were anything like the ones back on Earth, the people who had to work would be none too happy.

Looking into the mirror, she frowned at the dark blue dress she was wearing. It was made of a chiffon-like material. Unfortunately, her clothes were replaced daily, and she had no choice but to wear whatever was laid out for her. It was frustrating, and she knew that if she did get an opportunity to leave this place, this particular outfit would certainly not help her in that endeavor. It was completely impractical with its sleeveless, low-cut design. The only thing resembling warmth was a light shawl she had been given for her shoulders. The dress hung down to her ankles, and she could barely see her shoes from underneath it. No doubt it would snag on every branch and bush along whatever escape route she tried to take. She could probably cut it to a shorter length as she had done with the outfit she had received from Daric before being brought here. That thought brought with it a wave of emotion. Daric and her father...what were they doing right now? Maybe they believed her to be dead. Surely they must know that it was Vasin who had her? The not knowing was the most difficult, and in the end she knew she could not wait for rescue. She must find the courage to help herself.

She sighed and shook her head, looking down. Despite the impracticality of the piece, it did flatter her figure well, and she supposed looking a little pretty couldn't hurt, could it? And most important, she'd at least been able to craft an ad-hoc pocket underneath the many skirt layers to hide Shalin; the book was snug and out of view. She took one final look then turned toward her bedroom door.

As she left her room and walked down the long hallway toward the stairs, she could hear the muffled sound of the music below her. As she neared the first step of the stairway, the song became clear; it was entrancing. It had a light and quick melody that also managed a complex musical blend.

She walked down the stairs and toward the great hall. As she crossed the threshold, she could see that it had been transformed. Decorations draped every wall and window. They were all rich in autumn colors of brown, orange, red, and gold. Autumn-dedicated statues had been carved out of wood and placed in various spots throughout the room. Most of the carvings were more three-dimensional designs as opposed to actual people or things. They were beautiful and intricate. She had been told that they were symbols of the fall harvest. She thought that this seemed similar to perhaps a wreath or a tree symbolizing Christmas.

She could now see the source of the music. It was a group of musicians playing in the far left corner of the hall. The room had the perfect architecture to help richen the acoustics of every note. Except for one woman, who was playing something that looked very much like a piano, the other six musicians all played unfamiliar instruments. Seeing the piano brought an unexpected twinge of nostalgia to Sara. She herself had learned to play as a child. Her father had taught her. They had played together often and even done several recitals. It had been a much simpler time; it was a time she most definitely missed. She looked farther over and noticed that Balu, along with several other children including Farica and Taban, were gathered together in a loose circle, all dancing. They moved, in part, to the music, but also to their own innermost tune. They lived in an uninhibited and free time of their life. How she admired and longed for that same liberation. Suddenly, Balu saw her, stopped dancing, and headed toward her. He waved as he walked over. She couldn't help but wave back.

He reached her and said, "Hello, Sara!"

"Hi, Balu. Are you having fun?"

"Yes!" He seemed, instantly, to remember something. He put his hand in his pocket, felt around, and then pulled it back out. He held his hand out to her, at first balled up into a fist, but then he uncurled his fingers—her pearl ring! "It's my festival gift to you!"

"Balu! How did you get it back?"

"Well, I traded it, of course."

"But with what?"

Balu shook his head and refused to say. It must have been something very valuable with what she'd been able to trade for it in the first place.

Sara pulled him to her and hugged him tightly, small tears beginning to well up in her eyes. "Thank you, Balu."

She released him, and he turned, running back to his friends.

She walked over to a huge, rectangular wooden table. It was a seemingly new addition to the room and was where everyone would eat for each of the celebrations. It looked as though it could easily seat over a hundred people. Although no one was sitting down just yet, it was handsomely set with gold-colored dishes and goblets and the most intricately designed tablecloth she'd ever seen. It looked hand stitched and had not only elaborate designs but also story-scapes embroidered into the cloth. Where the table was not decorated it was covered with food. They'd already brought out trays of meats, fruits, vegetables, cheeses, and breads.

Vasin had requested that she sit next to him during the first night of harvest celebrations. He, of course, sat at the head of the table, and she could see her seat just to his right. She was leery of this but felt as if she had no choice but to comply.

She started to notice that the other people standing nearby were stealing subtle glances and looking at her with almost reverent eyes. She felt a very strong urge to run away, but the best she could do for the moment was to fantasize about how she might escape through the immense glass doors leading out to the balcony. It was as she looked just to the right of those doors that she saw him. Aron was standing against the wall and talking with three guards. It was the first time she'd seen him since the day they had arrived to Valina, and it was surreal. How often might one see a kidnapper at a dinner party after an abduction? But there he was...and there something about him. Even though she wanted to hate him for bringing her here, there was a powerful presence about him that she could not ignore. It most definitely set her emotions on edge, and she stood there paralyzed, unable to move forward. As if feeling her stare, he looked over, and their eyes met for just a moment. She looked away quickly, feeling flustered. Out of the corner of her eye, she thought she saw him starting to cross the hall in her direction. Was he coming over? She couldn't look. She suddenly felt very uncomfortable. Sara had connected with him in a strange way on the journey to Valina.

Her thoughts were interrupted.

Vasin stood before her with his hand outstretched. "Sara, come with me. I'd like to introduce you to some people." She let him take her arm and lead her across the room.

Sara stood next to Vasin for several minutes while he introduced her to three of his "advisers," as he called them. The jobs of those men seemed similar to positions back on Earth. The first man, she learned, was in charge of the palace guards and the sentries who were sent outside the city. Apparently this was a newer position that had arisen out of the dispute between Vasin and her father. The second man kept track of the city's overall health and social needs. He ensured that the people had the support that they needed—food, clothing, housing, and education. Sara likened it to a supplemental social welfare system. The people lived on their own, but the city provided for them if they could not provide for themselves. The third man was in charge of ensuring civil order, a police chief of sorts. She would have thought that a role like that was unnecessary in Valina.

"I thought that Valina did not have issues associated with crime," she asked the man.

He responded, "This position is a new one, specifically requested by Vasin himself. Unfortunately, we have seen a recent rise in *incidents*."

"What types of incidents?" she asked innocently.

"Mainly assault, but we've also, unfortunately, seen more domestic abuse."

"Oh no, that's terrible." And she truly meant it.

"Well, the good news is that we don't have to deal with such violent crimes such as murder."

Sara noted that the man conveniently left out the murders occurring as the result of the fight between Vasin and her father. This included their own planned murder of her. Why was Vasin treating her like an honored guest when his ultimate goal was to kill her? None of this made sense to her. She hated him for how nonchalant and normal he was acting. There was nothing ordinary or typical about her life right now.

A bell rang, signaling that dinner was to begin. Fortunately, it broke her out of her trance.

Sara took her seat along with the many others. The room quickly quieted, and Vasin stood up from his seat to address the group. He held up his hand palm up and gestured as he spoke. "I would like to give thanks for this autumn season, this time of change for Valina. It is change that will ensure the safety of our city and our planet. And last, I would like say thanks for Sara who has come here to help us."

Everyone began to clap as he said those last words, and she watched as the people looked from Vasin to her. They knew. They knew what Vasin was planning.

Vasin sat down, and with that, dinner commenced. There were pleasant conversation and happy faces all around her. She, however, barely touched her food and focused on maintaining her composure next to her soon-to-be executioner. Dinner passed in a blur, and if she'd been in a better place with her thoughts and her overall situation, it would have been difficult not to truly enjoy herself.

About an hour after dinner, though most still sat amicably talking at the large table, Sara had regained her wits and decided it was time to start her inspection of fortress walls that surrounded Valina. She stood up from her seat at the table and walked inconspicuously toward the exit at the front of the hall. No one was paying much attention to her at this point, as the newness of her presence had worn off, and the night's festivities were beginning to kick into full gear. Walking through the heavy, oversize doors that led out of the hall, she started down a set of nearby side stairs that she hoped would lead her down into the city streets. The area around her got darker as she descended the stairs, so much so that she was having a hard time seeing the steps below her.

As Sara came around the corner and down the last step, which dropped her just outside of the main palace and into the shadows of a nearby alleyway, she ran unexpectedly into two of the city men. Both of them smelled of sweat, and they acted almost inebriated in their mannerisms. She remembered what one of Vasin's advisers had said about some crime still existing. Her instincts also told her *trouble*. Either way she most certainly was not going to give them the benefit of the doubt. She started to turn back toward the way she had come, but before she could, one of the men grabbed her wrist roughly and said, "And where do you think you're going?"

Stunned, she struggled out of his grip and moved away from him, only to have the other man push her up against the wall and hold her there. Fear and shock started to take hold of her. It was very dark, and she could barely see two feet in front of her. He kissed her roughly, bruising her lips. She gasped and attempted to escape, but his hold was strong. She could not believe this was happening. Fate could not be this cruel.

Then, as rapidly as the whole situation had began, it ended. She could not see, but rather heard, a struggle in the shadows. The man accosting her heard it, too, because he turned, still holding her against the wall, and looked for the source of the sound. Then all of a sudden his grip loosened on her, and he slowly crumpled to the ground. She heard her rescuer curse and then slowly come from out of the shadows. It was Aron. He was breathing hard, and he ran his hand through his hair. He looked so angry.

"You shouldn't be here."

She couldn't stop the tears that started welling up in her eyes, "I'm sorry. I know."

He softened a little and touched her shoulder. "Are you OK?"

Shakily she responded, "Yes, thank you. If you hadn't come when you did…well…"

Bewildered and still shocked, she couldn't stand there any longer, and she couldn't say anymore. She turned swiftly and started back up the stairs toward the main hall.

CHAPTER 6

A VISIT WITH HECATE

To some they are just the ramblings of an
old woman; to others they might just
be the song of our future.

"Balu, are you sure this is the way?"

Sara and Balu had been walking through the back alleys and darker areas of the city for close to thirty minutes.

"Yes, yes. We're almost there." Balu smiled and kept walking.

She was pretty sure that no one knew of this trip except Balu, and she felt empowered by that. She'd gone to great lengths to ensure that Vasin did not know of her whereabouts this time.

Balu stopped abruptly, causing Sara to bulldoze right into him, knocking them both to the ground.

"We're here!" he exclaimed, still lying on the ground.

"We're here? I don't see anything."

Balu stood up, dusting off his pants. He pointed very matter-of-factly and said, "See, right over there."

Sara followed his finger down the stone street toward a very small, dark alleyway. At first she didn't see anything, but then as her eyes focused she saw a very small building. She suddenly felt herself lose her courage to go farther. Balu offered his hand in a gesture to help her up and to bolster her bravery. She accepted the offer, and once she was up on two feet he started to shove her, less tenderly now, toward the entrance.

"Go. Go. She'll be expecting you," he said.

"You told her about my visit?"

"No, but she knows things. Don't worry." He moved to a small wooden bench to the right of the door. "I'll wait here."

Sara inched toward the entrance and knocked quietly.

"Come in, Sara, my dear," said an old and wise voice.

Not knowing how this woman knew her name or her visit, Sara slowly pushed open the door. It was smoky and dark in the hut. Sara would not have guessed that it was the middle of the afternoon with the sun shining just outside the alleyway. No, she had entered into another world. It was the world of this woman. Out of the dark backdrop emerged the old woman. She hobbled up to Sara, grabbed her right hand with both of hers, patted it, and said, "My child, welcome—welcome. Please sit."

Sara did as she was told and sat on a stool near the fireplace. She watched as the old lady meandered over to the fireplace with a pot and slowly hung it from a wire just a few inches above the licking flames. Once she was satisfied that her task was complete, Hecate the healer turned to Sara and said, "So, you have come to ask questions of me, have you? So, ask them. Ask!"

Sara, took a deep breath and figured she might as well get right to the point. "Well, I was wondering if you could help me...escape Valina."

"Escape Valina?" Hecate asked, sounding surprised. "Now, why would you ever want to do that?"

Very disappointed, Sara responded, "Because I don't belong here. I need to get back to my family. I need to get back to my home."

"I think we should start from the beginning. You need to understand how this all started with your family."

Sara wasn't exactly sure what Hecate meant by that, but she sat quietly waiting for the woman to begin the story.

"Your father, Kalen, and Vasin are brothers."

"What?" Sara was in shock. "That can't be. They're enemies."

Hecate continued as if Sara had said nothing. "Their father's name was named Aylmer, and he was the leader of our world."

Sara interrupted again. "I can't believe that they are brothers."

"Vasin is eight years older than Kalen. Their mother tragically and unexpectedly died in childbirth with Kalen. It affected Vasin greatly as a boy."

"I'm sorry, but I thought that type of thing didn't happen here with the people's healing abilities."

"My child, it is true that our advances in medicine and our connection to Esereth have allowed us the ability to all but eradicate unnatural death. What happened with Vasin and Kalen's mother was very, very rare. And as a result of that fact, I believe it made it more difficult for Vasin to accept. He was just a boy."

"Hecate, are you a healer?"

Hecate nodded and looked at Sara, saying, "Yes, and I have been for one hundred years."

In her head, Sara did the mental time conversion between Earth and Esereth and responded, "Hecate, that's over one thousand years on Earth!"

Hecate nodded in agreement. She continued the story. "The boys were close to one another when they were young, despite the age difference. They were always getting into trouble, always finding some way out of it with their quick wits and adventurous spirits.

It was only once they reached adulthood that their views started to shift, and after Aylmer's death they fought constantly."

Hecate moved from near the fireplace and sat in a chair next to the table. Every step toward the chair appeared to pain her, but she still continued, intent on the relief that her destination would provide.

Once seated she said, "I am no longer young and need to rest. If you come back some other time, I will tell you the rest of their story."

"No, please!" Sara begged. "I'm sorry, but I need to hear it now."

"No, no, come back tomorrow."

Hecate said this with such a tone of finality that Sara knew it would do no good to argue. She nodded, disappointed, exiting into the alley. The more information she learned, the more disturbed she became. She needed to learn the whole truth if she was to continue in this place. It was all so complicated and so very confusing.

Sara came back the next day, without Balu this time, but Hecate was not there. She asked a man who lived next door where Hecate might have gone. The man thought she had left the city for a few days, and that was all he knew. Sara was utterly frustrated. She did not have time to wait. She very slowly made her way back to the palace, wondering how she was going to escape. She had not yet figured out her plan but felt still that Hecate might be able to help her. She wasn't sure how, but the woman was special.

∽

Aron stood guard on the wall. It was his turn in the rotation for the night shift. He stood alongside of one other man. It was custom not to speak to each other unless addressing an issue or a problem, and as a result, it left them often to their own thoughts.

Aron had become more and more concerned with Vasin's recent actions. He was conflicted, because Vasin had always been good to him and had always been a just man. He'd helped him and had trained him how to be a leader and a fighter. And when Vasin had told him that there was to be a girl named Sara, from Earth, who would be their savior, he had believed him unequivocally and jumped at the opportunity to serve.

But something was changing. He had been surprised when Vasin had told him that he must kidnap Sara and bring her to Valina, but Aron had dutifully followed orders. Now Vasin had Aron working day and night to find Shalin. Vasin believed that without having both Shalin and Sara together, he could not truly disconnect the bridge, and therefore, the fate of the people. Aron did what he could to find the book, but they had no leads on its whereabouts. Vasin had been outraged and upset with the lack of progress, so much so that he had several of his men beaten. Aron had never seen him lose his temper in that way; it stunned him that Vasin would hurt any of the people of Valina. Aron saw that Vasin was getting more frustrated and more extreme with every day that passed. More and more he felt as though he was actually watching the man he had known most of his life change right before his eyes. He did not like what he saw.

∽

The next week a routine developed for Sara. Each morning she had awakened to a knock at her bedroom door—her makeshift alarm clock. An older woman with long gray hair would enter with clean clothes for Sara, a basin of warm water for washing, and a small breakfast tray. After washing and dressing she would head down the stairs and just outside the palace to meet Balu. They wandered the city streets, exploring most of each day. Part of the daily city circuit was to walk past Hecate's house. Every day, so far, Sara was disappointed anew. Hecate had still not come back.

After returning to the palace, Sara spent some time resting in her room before dinner. The gray-haired woman consistently left a new tray with a small, single black cup and a teapot-like kettle filled with a dark red, hot liquid Sara thought reminded her of hibiscus tea. She'd traveled briefly to Egypt with her mother as a teenager, and they'd tried it while there. It was a nice memory. Sara had been lucky enough with the weather to take her tea on the balcony.

Every night dinner was provided as an informal meal in the main hall. It wasn't like that night of the large autumn festival. It was more of an informal buffet-type dinner. She, Balu, Farica, and Taban filled their plates and then headed back to Sara's room to eat. Every night while down in the hall, she'd secretly looked for Aron. She justified it by telling herself that she only wanted to thank him for his help that night against her attackers, but it was a hard sell, even to herself.

Her last routine of each day was a walk along the city wall. It took close to an hour to circumnavigate the entire distance. She wasn't sure what she was looking for but hoped that somehow knowledge of her cage could help her to find a way to escape. And as much as she was starting to feel an attachment to this place, she had not forgotten that she was its prisoner.

༄

Tonight, Sara made her way back to the palace from the wall and had just reached the marketplace, which marked the halfway point between the wall and the palace. She walked briskly; the bottoms of her shoes on the rocky dirt made a grinding sound each time she stepped. The vendors had shutdown their booths and gone home hours ago, and it felt very lonely and unwelcome to her to be passing through there now.

She suddenly heard a man yelling. He likely wasn't yelling very loudly, but the sound in contrast to the silent streets made it seem as though he was screaming. Her path back to the palace seemed to be taking her directly to the source of the commotion.

She now saw two men standing just inches from one another in the middle of the street, fists clenched. Their contempt for one another was obvious. She heard one man accuse, "This is all your fault."

The other man retorted, "Me? You were the one that made the agreement." That same man pushed the other man causing him to lose his balance and fall to the ground. The accosted man looked livid. He jumped up and pushed back. They grabbed one another almost simultaneously on the shoulders and began to wrestle. She did not know what the fight was about, but she could see that it was escalating. Sara quickly stepped onto a side street that would take her a block over and away from the dispute. There was nothing she could do, and she definitely did not want to stick around to find out how it all turned out. She picked up her pace to a light jog, making record time back to the palace. She thought, "What was happening to these people?"

❦

It was a full week before Sara was able to track down Hecate again—or rather, until Hecate decided to find Sara.

Sara walked along the main floor of the palace with Ifan. He was taking her to the great hall so she could see the preparations that had been made so far for the second of the large celebrations. She had not realized it during the first gala, but each of the three celebrations had its own theme. The first had been what she would have imagined a fall festival to be, with the autumn-dedicated colors and symbols. The second was supposed to include more of a winter theme. However, the third, she was told, was always a surprise for the people. She couldn't help but be intrigued.

As they entered the great hall, Sara looked over and saw the most beautiful array of blue banners and streamers along the walls and draped from the high ceiling. They were made out of a soft velvet-like material that provided a rich texture and accentuated the different shades of color. Several men and women were in the process of hanging white silk-like lanterns from the ceiling. She imagined it would be especially beautiful once the sun went down.

She looked toward the back of the hall at the entrance on the other side of the expanse and let out a surprised grunt that she could not manage to stifle. It was loud enough that Ifan noticed, too, and looked to see what she had reacted to. Hecate was slowly ambling across the hall toward Sara. It took her several minutes to achieve her goal, and Sara and Ifan said and did nothing as she approached. The woman surprised Sara further by giving her a tightly gripped hug once she got close enough. It was a hug that might have been shared by two longtime friends.

During the hug she said in a low voice, "Meet me at my home...dusk."

Then she patted Sara on the arm and turned to hobble out of the hall. Ifan told Sara that he'd never seen Hecate in the great palace—ever.

Later that day she made her way to Hecate's. She turned her attention to the people around her as she walked. She'd been doing a lot of that lately—watching how they worked, how they interacted with one another, and how they treated one another. To her knowledge there weren't any hardened "criminals" in Valina. She had seen problems, as she had observed on the first night of the festival with her attackers, as well as the fight she had recently witnessed on her way back from the wall, but things like mass murders and extremely violent crimes just didn't seem to happen here. It almost seemed impossible for this peace to be true, at least based on her experiences on Earth, but Balu had further verified pieces of similar information. She had asked him about the cell where she had been tucked away. He'd responded that the main palace was very old. It was built when the city was built, which was over five hundred years ago. He wasn't quite sure what purpose those rooms had held at the palace's beginning. It seemed improbable, but somehow there was no need for a prison in Valina.

Before Sara even had a chance to knock on Hecate's door, she heard, "Come in!"

How did Hecate know that she was here? Sara shook her head in amazement and slowly entered, waiting again for her eyes to adjust. Hecate was sitting in the same chair as she had been when Sara had left the last time. It was all familiar. It was like the continuation of a dance, and they were picking up with their last step.

"So, you would like me to finish my story?" Hecate asked.

"Very much," Sara responded.

"Would you like something to drink?"

"No, thank you, Hecate."

Hecate seemed not to hear her as she set a cup of very dark liquid before Sara. "What is it?" Sara wondered. She picked up the drink and brought it closer to her. She crinkled her nose. It had a strong, almost leather-like smell. Was this really to drink? She dared not ask, and out of extreme politeness, she took a small sip. It was bitter, but thank goodness, not as horrible as her nose had just prophesied.

"So, where were we?" asked Hecate. Before Sara had a chance to respond, Hecate picked up the thought on her own. "Ah, yes. I remember now. Aylmer, Vasin and Kalen's father, had just died. Why were the two sons fighting? you might ask. Well, just before Aylmer died, he passed on to them the knowledge that supposedly lies within the book, Shalin. Aylmer and his line had been keepers of the known knowledge of the book since the key's mysterious disappearance over two hundred years ago."

"So that explains a little more about the book and the key," Sara mentally noted.

"Each generation would pass on what they knew just before death," Hecate continued. "The majority of the knowledge is never to be known by anyone except the keepers, but there are bits and pieces, as they become relevant to all of us, that the leaders disseminate to the people. There is a strong, unquestioning belief in the book and its prophesies."

Sara asked, "Why do people not question?"

"Well," Hecate responded, "Shalin has foretold many events correctly. And in doing so it has helped the people of Esereth to live as they do today. They remain connected to one another and to this planet. Information about the two planets' past and their connections to each other is one such example. The book is also where the people of Esereth have gotten all their healing knowledge."

Sara had to all but bite her tongue to keep from asking the thousand questions that had just popped into her head with that bit of information, but she knew that it didn't work that way. It was up to Hecate to tell her what she needed to know.

"Kalen and Vasin believed very differently about how to handle the book's information passed on to them from their father. Vasin believed in trying to change that fate. He wanted to control it at all costs. Kalen took on his father's philosophy of accepting the fate that the book foretold, no matter what it might bring. It's hard to say why Vasin was so intent on controlling and changing the outcome of the book's predictions. Some say it was the loss of his mother. It created a fear in him, and a need to control at all costs." Hecate paused and shook her head in sadness. "Others have said it is because of something that he had learned from Aylmer and the book."

Then Hecate said something that surprised Sara. "Two years after their father's death, Kalen took the book and fled to Earth."

"Wait, you're saying my father stole Shalin?"

"He took the great book because Vasin threatened to destroy it. Through destruction of the book, Vasin was trying to sever the link between our two worlds—our two universes. Kalen would not let that happen, and so he spent several years hiding on Earth with the book."

Sara sucked in her breath at the mention of this part of the story; this was where she entered the picture.

Hecate continued, "Vasin searched continuously for your father and the book, and finally he did the one thing he knew would bring your father back with the book to Esereth. He threatened war. War has been nonexistent on Esereth, and to even think of it was unspeakable. Vasin knew just the threat of it would bring your father back to Esereth."

With that last information, Sara felt a very small part of her inwardly heal. As much as losing her father had devastated her as a child, there was some comfort in understanding this bigger picture.

Hecate continued, "So, as expected, Kalen returned." She grabbed Sara's hand, leaned in, and then said, "Your father's visit to Earth caused some-thing truly unexpected to happen. It created a living link between our two universes...you, Sara."

Sara shook her head in disbelief. "Hecate, who's right? Vasin or my father?"

"You must answer that. That is why you are here. You are the one who will help lead us on our true path."

"No, it can't be me," Sara immediately replied.

"Make no mistake," Hecate said in a tone that made the hair on Sara's neck stand on edge, "you are the one— born half of Esereth, half of Earth. You have connected the universes in a very special way."

"I can't be the only one who has ever been from both planets! Not as long as they've been connected." But it came out more as a question than a statement.

Hecate paused, shaking her head as if remembering something troubling, "There was one other, a very long time ago, who was like you."

"Who?" Sara asked.

Hecate did not answer her question but said, "You *must* figure out your role in this, Sara—for the sake of us all."

༖

"Where is the book?" Daric asked.

Kalen did not answer.

It was just past dawn and Kalen and Daric walked along the camp perimeter to survey the preparation for the soldiers' training activities planned for the day. The sky, all around them, was a sheet of hot pink. It provided an unlikely combination of both shadowed and iridescent tones.

"Is Shalin safe? Is it here on Esereth or still on Earth?" Daric pushed harder for some sort of information.

"It is here on Esereth. I gave the book to someone I trust after I returned from Earth."

Kalen knew that as long as Vasin did not have the book, they at least had a chance. He also knew that he could not keep it. It was much too dangerous. There was only one woman who would know what to do to keep it out of Vasin's hands.

This seemed to satisfy Daric for the time being.

Kalen changed topics, "The plans for Sara are making progress."

Kalen could see Daric physically tense up. He knew Daric was very emotionally invested in this rescue. It was also why Kalen had led the plans and not directly involved Daric, at least not yet.

Kalen continued, "We heard word yesterday that we were able to get one of our men into Valina."

Daric asked, "How did you do it?"

"We were able to have him integrate with a large group of men who were participating in a training exercise near the outskirts of the city. He posed as someone from one of the nearby villages loyal to Valina. They accepted him into the group. He will be key in helping us when the time comes to enter the city."

"That's very good news," Daric responded.

"The pieces have been put into place, and we will ride in two weeks' time to bring Sara back to us."

Kalen noted that the vibrant colors that had enveloped the sky were already starting to fade. The sun was rising up above the horizon, forcing everything to be seen in full light. He hoped that the people could all live with what they saw; the light of day would soon be upon Esereth.

ESCAPE ATTEMPT

Nobody can escape the consequences of his choices.

Sara's hand had involuntarily started to shake, and her heart, well, it felt as though it could literally jump through her chest. She forced herself to take a deep breath and to steady herself. The anxiety she felt at the possibility that she might actually attempt to do this was extreme. But she knew that if she was to attempt to escape Valina on this night, she'd need to maintain complete control.

The opportunity had presented itself when she'd least expected it. She'd gone out for her evening walk along the wall of the city. It was a narrow walkway at the top of the wall that circled the entire city. The inner side of the walkway and the outer wall were about twelve feet higher above her, but every several hundred feet or so there was a large opening where a guard could sit and take watch. Through that opening a person could lean over to view the forest and moat-like river that surrounded the city. The people who manned these locations were alert sentries of some sort.

Sara had hoped—no, dreamed—that something like this might happen. As she'd walked past one of these openings, she'd seen that one of the wall guards was not at his station, and she'd waited, watching expectantly for the guard to reappear, but he had not. Handovers between men overlapped so as to never leave a gap in attendance at the post, but this station, for whatever reason, was vacant. She knew the consequences of being caught were deadly and had realized with both excitement and apprehension that this was her chance. Despite all that she had learned over the last several weeks and the relationships that she had started to build with some of the people here, she knew that if she stayed in Valina she would still come to the same end—dead. Valina would be her undoing, and her father and Daric her salvation. She must find them.

She mentally cursed because her bag of supplies was back in her room, and there was no telling how long the guard post would remain vacant. She couldn't risk ruining her one chance of escape; she would have to go without them. She'd never expected that she might actually have a spontaneous opportunity to escape from the wall, only that she might find information she needed for a future escape.

Hugging her back against the high stone wall of the city, she inched her way toward the vacated guard post. It was just past dusk, and the darkened sky camouflaged her. She could feel her excitement starting to build. She might just make this work. She knew if she could get to the opening, she could make the jump off the wall ledge into the water that surrounded it. The distance from the ledge to the water at this point was probably fifty feet at most. She'd made crazy dives like this as a teenager, from a small cliff near her grandmother's home, but never at night and never into water that was likely more shallow. She had no choice but to believe, though, that she could make the jump and not break every bone in her body.

It was time. She stood now on the ledge that overlooked the open expanse of blackness. She sucked in a deep breath, took one step forward, and plunged into the dark abyss below.

She knew that both the distance of the jump and the autumn-chilled water were going to be a formidable challenge, but nothing could have prepared her for the shock of it all. After breaking through the stinging barrier of water from the initial jump, her survival instincts kicked in, and she attempted to swim up and break through the icy-cold dark barrier to gulp her first breath of air. But where there should have been air, there was more water. Her attempt at a second breath did not yield better results. She was now striving to utilize every last brain cell she had to prevent herself from panicking. She knew that if she could not hold it together, she would very quickly drown. She attempted, unsuccessfully, to stroke forward, but it seemed to be useless. She knew at best she was treading water and getting nowhere. She could already start to feel her hands going numb, but she told herself severely to push through it. Her silent punishment allowed her to bring her head briefly above the horizon of water. She caught a glimpse of the embankment which was only several feet away, but it might well have been a million miles. The chill of the water was now causing her to lose command of her limbs. This lack of control caused her head to go back underwater at the same time she was attempting a breath of air. She knew it as much as she felt it—she was beginning to drown.

The water had grown arms and was pulling her down even farther. She had always morbidly wondered how she would go, how she would transition from this life into the next, but she'd always been sure she would be ready for it. She'd assumed it would be once she had finished up her work in this life, and she knew at this moment that that fact could not be true. There were too many questions unanswered. Too many things she had yet to accomplish. And even as her anger at these thoughts gave her an additional burst of energy, she knew that she was not strong enough to make it. She was not strong enough to live.

∽

Aron had led the night's patrol around the outskirts of Valina. They went out every evening now, searching for Kalen's men. This concept of defensive patrols, sentries, and offensive attacks against Kalen and his men was not the nature of the people. All had lived their entire lives in peace, and it hadn't been until the last few years that everything had changed. It saddened him deeply that things had turned to this fear and fighting.

He'd watched the transition of the people as well. They were more afraid now. They trusted others less. He'd also noticed that crimes in the city were getting worse. And who was he kidding? He'd been a part of that transition. Teaching the men how to handle weapons, working strategies for attacks, drilling into them the more paranoid behavior required of people who have an enemy.

He'd had a group of four men with him this night, but he had let them all go back to the city ahead of him. They should be allowed to enjoy the time with their families and friends. Aron had finished the evening alone without issues or new findings and was now on his way back to the city. Every day brought winter closer, and it was obvious that the recent nights had already yielded to the unbending grip of it. The wind tonight was harsh and felt every bit of winter. He himself was very much looking forward to getting home and out of this weather. He could even see the gate in the distance now. He eagerly urged his brown mare from a walk into a trot toward the entrance, knowing that saving himself even a few minutes of this cold would be worth the effort.

As he approached the moat surrounding Valina, he heard what he thought might have been the sound of splashing. It was barely audible over the sounds of the horse's hooves, and so he almost missed it. He slowed his horse to a walk to listen more intently. Aron strained to look into the moat for some sign that he had not been hearing things. Then he saw it. There was movement in the water. He cursed to himself quickly, sliding off of his horse. He did not know how it was possible, but some fool had jumped into the water and was likely drowning. He accelerated from walk to jog toward the embankment. He looked with difficulty into the black void of water. Suddenly, he caught the glimmer of a familiar face just before it was taken below into darkness.

"No. It can't be," he thought. "Sara?"

Without another moment's delay, he dove into the icy waters. Expertly he swam to the place where he had last seen her and dove below the surface. He found her not by sight or feel, but by sheer luck. It was a miracle that she had not yet sunk too far below the surface. He quickly wrenched Sara up so that her head was out of the water and then swam expertly, with her pulled closely to him, to the water's edge. After pulling them both out of the water, he lay next to her unmoving body while he himself breathed heavily from the cold and the strain of it. She looked so pale in the moonlight, her dress clinging to her lifeless body.

"She can't be dead," he thought.

He leaned next to her face and listened for breathing. There was nothing. He felt her neck. There was only a faint pulse. There was little time, but he believed he could still save her. He stood up and then quickly retrieved a small pack that was attached to the saddle of his horse. From it he pulled a small vial with the expected green glow, and he gave her a small amount, pouring it down her throat. Within seconds she was coughing up water. He wasted no time. He pulled a small utility blanket from his horse and covered her shoulders with it. Aron then quickly mounted his horse, bringing her up with him so that she was facing him, her arms loosely draping his waist. He would have to take her back through Valina's walls and to his own home, but he could not let Vasin know she was here. The only conclusion he could come to was that she had tried to escape. Vasin's response would be severe.

Sara was still unconscious and limp in his arms as they entered the city gates. Instinctively, Aron pulled her closer to him, so close that he could feel her shallow breath against his cheek. This small sign of life kept him from going mad. She was not supposed to mean this much to him. He was aching with the thought that she might have died tonight. And he knew that she was not completely out of harm's way. He would have to watch her closely throughout the night.

No one paid them heed as he entered Valina. It was late, and he often came through at all hours of the night after patrolling. The people had come to trust everything about him. He had helped to build and protect their city. This night he was thankful for that fact.

He lived on the outer edge of the city and so they were back at his home within only a few minutes after entering the walls. He slid off his horse, not bothering to even tether it to the post that was right outside his door. Cradling Sara in his arms, he kicked the door open with his foot and immediately felt a welcome burst of warm air. The fire he had left before heading out to patrol was almost gone, but it had left for him a heated hut. He laid her onto a large brown rug on the floor in front of the fireplace. This transition from his arms to the floor caused her to stir, and he decided to take that opportunity to try to call her back to him.

"Sara...listen to me. You're safe. Don't try to move."

She was still so pale.

He quickly stripped off her wet clothes and wrapped her in warm blankets that he had taken from his bedchamber. Then something happened. As he moved her dress from the floor to the nearby table, Shalin fell from the hidden pocket onto the floor.

He jerked back as if having been burned. He was shocked. She had the book! "How long has she had *that?*" he thought.

A light moan of pain came from her lips, and he was reminded of the current situation. He would have to deal with that information later. As he turned toward her, he could see that she was shivering badly now, still not coherent. He put the book back into the dress pocket that it had fallen from and swiftly walked back over to Sara. He took off his own cold, wet tunic, chest now bare, and then bent over her, pulling her to him, his skin now touching hers. He sat down with her in his arms against the wall next to the hearth of the fireplace and held her tightly.

Almost an hour later, her eyes fluttered open, and she stared at him. She started to push herself from his arms.

"No, stay here. You're safe now. Just don't move," he said.

This struggle seemed to take what little strength she had built up, and she fell back unconscious in his arms.

The physical closeness between them was impossible to ignore. She was beautiful and frail. He noted the contrast between her ivory skin and his own, weathered and tanned. He spent the rest of the night cradling her next to the fire. It wasn't until the light of the morning that he was satisfied she would make it through this harrowing ordeal. With a sigh he finally allowed himself to drift into a dreamless sleep.

❧

Sara felt the ache of her entire body before she even thought to open her eyes.

"Am I dead?" she thought.

She hadn't supposed that death would feel so horrible. At least she had hoped it wouldn't. She finally opened her eyes and was surprised to see that it was no longer dark outside and that, in fact, she was being partially blinded by a ray of morning sunlight that shone through a window directly across from her. However, that was nothing compared to her astonishment to see that she was lying against a warm, male body. She was wrapped in Aron's arms, her head on his chest as he lay asleep in a sitting position against the wall of the hut. It all felt *much* too comfortable. She dared not move—not yet.

The night's events quickly spilled back into her head. She had failed. Her escape had failed. The realization of this disappointing knowledge made her heart sink. And yet somehow through all of this, she wasn't dead.

How had she gotten here? And with him?

She needed to leave this place, but she knew she didn't yet have the strength to move. So, instead she lifted her head just slightly and stared at him in awe and shock. She could feel his even breath and noticed how youthful and fragile he looked as he slept. It was nothing like when he was awake. He was so intimidating and hard when awake. She could not trust him. She knew why. He was her enemy. But then he had saved her and brought her here.

"Why didn't he bring me back to Vasin?" she thought. Her confusion had used up her small bit of energy, and with that last thought her exhaustion soon took over and she found herself drifting off again into sleep.

The next time she awoke she found herself not in Aron's arms but in a huge, dark brown wooden bed. She was breathing heavily and in a deep sweat. The dream she'd just been having was still fresh in her mind. It had all seemed so real. She immediately kicked her feet out from under the heavy fleece-like blankets that covered her and started to sit up. She was still very weak, and this was evident by the black spots that started to appear in front of her as she moved into the sitting position. She thought better of her recent actions and slowly lay back down.

In her dream she had been sitting quietly in a chair in the middle of the inner courtyard garden of the palace. The book was floating just in front of her face and was singing to her—singing to her in the same words that she had heard just before she had been transported to Esereth.

The words were emblazoned in her head: *"Transitio in lucem. Salvum planetarum."* They repeated to her over and over again. What did they mean? They seemed so real. Was it possible that that they were only something conjured up by her own imagination?

Despite her body's vehement protests, she sat up again and swung her feet down and over to the side of the bed; she needed to do something. She noticed that she wore only an oversize shirt; likely it was one of Aron's. She did not want to think about how he had gotten her into that. She raised herself from this sitting position and slowly shuffled her feet to the doorway and peeked around the corner. She had to lean against the doorframe for additional support. She saw Aron entering from outside with a stack of fresh firewood. He looked very tired and didn't notice her until she very quietly said his name.

"Aron."

He jolted at the soft sound of his name on her lips. Then he abruptly put down the stack of wood next to the fireplace and came toward her.

Gruffly he said, "You should not be up. You need to rest."

Sara felt like a small child being chastised and immediately thought to protest, but then thought better of it. She swallowed her pride, knowing that he had risked his life to save hers.

He softened. "Sara, we can talk about everything… later. You really need to get to bed. Let me help you."

She didn't argue and let him take her arm and guide her back to the bed. Even though it was only a few feet from her current location, the journey felt like miles. She was already starting to breathe heavily, and Aron saw this. Without asking he lifted her into his strong arms and carried her the rest of the way to the bed. She looked up at him, their eyes locking for a long moment. The look of intensity that he gave her troubled her immensely. She knew things had changed between them. His presence, now, was almost more than she could handle, and she knew that he was affected by her, too.

ଚ୨

She slept for several more hours. It was amazing what miracles rest alone could provide. As far as she could tell, he never left her, and that knowledge seemed to also have its own subtle healing capacity.

Later that afternoon, she exited the bedroom and sat down next to Aron, who was sitting just a few feet from the fire. They sat next to each other for several minutes without speaking. He finally broke the silence. "You must go back to the palace tonight. And we will need to provide a story to Vasin to explain where you've been."

"You would help me lie?"

He replied simply, "Yes."

"What should we say?" she asked.

"I could tell him that you were at Hecate's house. We'll need to talk with her as soon as possible, but I believe she would help you. She is very fond of you."

Aron stood up and said, "You should get dressed, and I'll go gather more firewood."

Sara walked back to the bedroom and over to the chest at the foot of the bed. Aron had left her dress there. It was dry now, and so she slipped it on. She noticed that Shalin was still hidden neatly inside the dress pocket.

She touched the book and thought, "Did he find it? Surely not. Surely he would have taken it from me." She let out a sigh of momentary relief; at least the book was still safe.

Sara went back to the palace, and with the help of Hecate very easily provided her story. Vasin had not seemed to even think twice about the story. It had all been too easy.

CHAPTER 8

THE CELEBRATION

Let us celebrate the upcoming winter wonder.

It had now been not quite a week since her escape attempt, and Sara hated to say it, but things had all but returned to normal. She wasn't sure how she could even use that word, considering everything that had happened since her receipt of Shalin, but her days had certainly regained their routine.

It was already close to midnight, but she was making her way down to the courtyard gardens to walk and think. There was a cobblestone walkway that connected the palace to the large oak tree in the center of the garden. That tree, which she had first seen from her room, was becoming an icon of refuge. She would sit on the wooden bench that sat in front of it and feel some sense of peace. The last leaves were still hanging on, not yet ready to take their final flight.

Sara was still weak from the escape attempt, but she'd been able to hide it well and after only a few days was feeling more like herself. She had not seen Aron since the day she had returned to Vasin, but as much as she tried she could not stop thinking about him.

At the sound of footsteps heading toward her, she jumped involuntarily. Her thoughts were abruptly put on hold as she assessed whether this person was friend or enemy. She turned toward the sound and saw that Ifan, her guard, was walking toward her. Ifan was an attractive young man who looked to be about twenty years old. That would make him a full eight years younger than herself. The last day or two he'd been with her more than ever, if that was possible. At first she'd thought that Vasin might have become suspicious, but as she now noted the look on Ifan's face as he approached her, a realization dawned on her. Ifan had also been looking at her a little differently lately. His stares lingered longer than was appropriate, and he had been "helping" her from place to place more frequently. She inwardly cringed at the full realization that he was smitten with her.

"This is just great," she thought sarcastically. One more thing to cause her problems.

Ifan reached her and lightly touched her arm, gesturing her up from the bench. "Sara, what are you doing out here so late?"

"Just...thinking," she responded. "Is there something wrong?"

Ifan responded, "No, no...it's just, well, it's never completely safe after dark. You need to be careful."

Ifan's eyes were now on the ground, but it didn't last long. He looked up as if remembering something, "I was told to tell you that Vasin will be saving you a seat again at the festival tomorrow tonight."

It wasn't really as if there was a choice, but it wasn't Ifan's fault. Sara smiled at him and said, "Thank you, Ifan. Tell him I will be there."

He nodded and then stood awkwardly, seeming to stare off into no place. His nervousness was starting to frustrate her. Finally, he came out with it, "Sara, I was wondering...well...if you would mind saving me a dance at the festival tomorrow?"

Sara took a deep breath, not altogether sure what to do. And as much as she wanted to say no to Ifan, she opted for noncommittal. "Well, we'll just have to see how the evening goes."

He seemed relieved to not have received blatant rejection and took that for the yes that it wasn't. He smiled widely, nodded, and started to back up, almost tripping on a potted plant that was sitting just off the garden path. Catching himself just barely, he turned around and headed back toward the doors.

One thing was for sure: the people of this city were becoming a part of her, and it scared her completely. These people were supposed to be her enemies, and instead they were asking her to save them a dance.

She was truly starting to wonder what reality was and who her enemies truly were.

That next night Sara headed down the main staircase in a gown that was a vibrant yellow color. It was sleeveless with shimmery white lace bordering the top. She had been given a light shawl to help with the chill. From the waist down it had several thin layers of a soft, almost fleece-like material. One of the ladies who worked at the castle, Linn, had been nice enough to braid Sara's hair earlier in the day. It was intricately done in a sort of complex French braid and then swept into a loose bun at the base of her neck with several wisps of hair free, delicately framing her face.

Sara, however, felt extremely uncomfortable—not physically, but mentally. She'd never really been the "done-up" type, and the tight-fitting, low curves of this garment certainly didn't make her feel any better. As she walked toward the great hall, her hand involuntarily swept toward the pockets under her skirt. She always had the book with her, and she'd felt the need more and more often to ensure that it was still safe. She was thankful that it was small and could be easily hidden under the large amount of material she was forced to wear. It was becoming a part of her, and there was a possessive, protective urge that was difficult to stifle. It was as if she was supposed to be its protector, and it needed her to maintain the story and the secrets of their two worlds that lay within it.

The music was familiar. Some of the tunes from the first festival were playing again, and she found herself humming the melodies on her own. It gave her a feeling of comfort. She approached the large wooden double doors and slowly walked through the entrance. The ambiance of the room immediately overwhelmed her. The decorations she had seen them preparing days earlier were now complete. The lit lanterns hung from the ceiling like stars, giving the hall a mysterious depth. The various shades of blue throughout complemented the overall emotion that the room invoked. The wooden sculptures, instead of autumn themed, were this time focused on the upcoming winter. It dawned on her that they were all snowflakes. There must have been at least twenty varieties, each its own unique pattern. It was all very beautiful.

She caught sight of Vasin already sitting at the great table. Seeing him triggered her feelings of dread and suspicion. She saw that there were people all around him except for the one promised empty seat that Ifan had mentioned. Sara cringed at the thought of having to sit next to Vasin again in this social environment. Ever since Hecate's shocking information that Vasin was her father's brother, her uncle, she was having a difficult time looking at him in the same way. How was it possible that this man wanted to do her harm? He must know that she was his niece, his blood relation.

Vasin caught sight of her and motioned his hand toward the empty seat to the right of him. Sara could not force herself to smile, but she did nod her head in acknowledgment of his gesture. She took her time walking over to the ornate, wooden, high-backed chair. She was in no hurry. To make things even more difficult, she was now seeing the physical similarities between Vasin and her father. They both had the same imposing height and frame, and they both had the same brown eyes—her eyes. It turned her stomach to think that this man, her captor, was any relation to the father she loved so much. She wished that she did not have to deal with this, but she steeled herself and continued the walk toward the table.

After she sat, he poured her a glass of what they called *shal* out of a tall, engraved glass decanter. Sara wasn't really sure what to think of the drink. It certainly made her feel like she did after a nice glass of red wine, although it was sweeter and had a thicker consistency. It struck her as oddly interesting that both worlds would have something like alcohol. It was perhaps the true medicine to society.

After moving the glass toward her, Vasin said, "Your father continues to try and stop me, but he does not understand what we must do, Sara. We must make sacrifices. He's always been naive like that, even when we were small boys. Sara, you must help me complete your destiny and the destiny of Esereth to disconnect the fates of our two worlds."

She'd been watching him speak. He was so sure of himself and the path that his people needed to take.

He continued, "I know you do not understand all of this, but you must believe that the sacrifice of your life is to allow the lives of the people on Esereth to continue. The life of one for the life of many."

"Even if I did, what of Earth?"

"This will allow the people of Earth to make their own destiny apart from ours."

It was silence between them now. She would not look at him. For the most part she believed that Vasin was a madman; however, lately there had been a small, nagging part of her suggesting the possibility that this man was right…that there was only one way to save the two worlds. Maybe he knew something that she and her father didn't. She'd seen a lot here that was the same as on Earth, but the path these people had taken was distinctly different. On some warped level, could there be a chance that what he said was true? Was it her selfish attachment to her own life that was biasing her view? Of course, not that anyone would blame her. And even if she did agree with him, how could she allow it? The consequences of either case were permanent. And what would that mean for the people of Earth? The reason that Vasin wanted to separate the two was because he did not trust that people on Earth would make the right decisions in the end. And she herself had felt that globally he was right: Earth *was* out of balance. The question was whether or not it was reparable, whether we, on Earth, could change our path.

After dinner she watched Vasin leave the great hall. He left with three other men from the city. She wondered, silently, where he was going.

Her attention shifted to a group of people who were gathering near the band. Couples started to dance. The melody felt very similar to a waltz. Ifan, to Sara's dismay, quickly came to her for what he interpreted as the promised dance. The boyish crush was now completely evident on his face. He looked back and forth from her to the ground, hands behind his back, and managed to eke out the words, "Sara, um, may…well, could I please…?"

Sara could see him starting to flush, and she had a flash of compassion. She sighed and surprising herself by saying, "Yes, Ifan."

He smiled widely and grabbed her hand, almost dragging her out onto the dance floor. She noticed that some of Ifan's friends were looking now with wide-eyed disbelief. It was obvious that they could not believe that Ifan had actually been successful in his quest. They looked upon him now with a newfound admiration.

There were already a great many people dancing, and it wasn't long before they were lost in the crowd of feet and bodies. Ifan was a good deal taller than she, and Sara had to tip her head up at an uncomfortable angle up to make eye contact. He seemed very proud of himself now and was starting to get a fresh wave of confidence—not usually good for a young man. It was becoming apparent that maybe she shouldn't have agreed to the dance. His hand started to move from her upper back to her lower. She had no desire to give him false hope, although under the circumstances she didn't feel like she had a lot of choice.

She started to pull away to end the dancing, but before she could, he surprised her by asking, "Sara, what's it like on Earth?"

This unexpected reminder of her home brought a smile to her face, and instead of walking away, she continued dancing with him and answered, "Well, things are really very similar to Esereth in many ways."

"In what ways are they not?"

"Well, one thing I see is that technology plays a much larger role for the people on Earth than here on Esereth. For instance, this hall and your homes are lit using fire, but the buildings and homes in certain places on Earth are lit using electricity."

He lifted one brow, looked down at her, and said skeptically, "And how exactly is it possible to illuminate with anything other than fire?"

"This is definitely going to take awhile," she thought.

Although she supposed that she hadn't much else better to do.

Three dances and an hour next to what could only be described as the "punch bowl" later, she had acquired a small crowd of avid listeners. She had transitioned to the discussion of natural resources, explaining as best she could the uses of coal, natural gas, and oil. She told them that millions of homes used natural gas to fuel stoves, furnaces, water heaters, clothes dryers, and other household appliances. She also discussed the recent evolution of regenerable energy such as solar power and wind energy. That one phrase had invoked a fury of additional questions. It surprised her how few of the details the people here really knew. It was notable that probably only a very small number of the population had the knowledge and experience of Vasin and her father.

All of these conversations caused her to reflect upon the people of Earth's ability to manipulate their natural environment into something new and different that met not only their needs but their wants. It was a simple fundamental fact that permeated every moment of their lives. From the time they woke up to the time they went to sleep, they were either using or creating tools. There were more revolutionary tool discoveries, such as the first manipulation of fire or the Internet, but even the more mundane items— toothbrush, pens, paper, houses, furniture, cars, phones. And as compared to Esereth, the people of Earth had taken things to a whole different level. They had gone past ready-to-hand tools and moved on to something much more complex. This had been both a blessing and a curse, and Sara knew that her planet was still working to find the balance of the power that these modern tools could provide. Sara did believe that the people of Earth would find this balance, but it would take time. From a macroscopic scale, humanity was probably only at best in the toddler phase of societal consciousness. And as such it was a critical and dangerous time, with no parent to guide and keep them safe from themselves. More than anything, humans needed time to mature.

There was something else that one of the boys had said in passing tonight that made her take pause and question the fundamental differences between the evolutionary path the people of Earth had taken versus the people of Esereth. Because the people of Esereth had never really known war, at least with no recent history to reference, they had never had the motivation that people on Earth had to make major strides in technology. It had been said that from the horror and death of World War II, some of the most amazing progress in technology of land, air, and power had also been made. Through death and power struggles, humans on Earth moved forward in technology. And because Esereth did not have these same motivations or experiences, they stood virtually still in time.

After all the deep thoughts, Sara was very thankful that this world had the wine equivalent of shal. She was starting to feel its warm delirium covering her, and that helped to lift the burden of her reality.

꙳

Aron had been watching her since she'd entered the hall for dinner. She was across the room now talking with several star-struck young men. They seemed to be intently listening as she animatedly explained something. She looked very beautiful tonight, having fully recovered from her near-death experience, and to see her out there dancing with Ifan both annoyed and maddened him. He knew it was more or less innocent, but he was amazed by how much she was affecting him. He'd been thinking about her almost nonstop, and the thought of anyone else…well, it was too much. He knew that before the end of the night he needed to at least speak to her—to touch her. And most important, tell her of his decision.

꙳

After begging rest from the stories about Earth, Sara walked toward the double glass doors leading to the balcony. The view out there was very similar to the view from her room. She leaned over the stone balcony a bit to better see the gardens. They spanned the entire circumference of the palace like a wreath.

She was alone out here. No one else seemed to care for the brisk air, and that was fine by her. She closed her eyes so that she could better feel the chilly air on her flushed face. She needed a moment of silence to gather her thoughts and control her wits.

She did not hear the figure that slowly walked up behind her in the darkness, and when she felt a touch on her arm, the surprise of it caused her to involuntarily jerk around and belt out the start of a pretty loud scream. The shriek was, however, stifled by a large, strong, familiar hand. Her breath caught as she turned around and saw that this hand belonged to Aron. He removed his hand from her mouth, but did not withdraw completely. He touched her cheek, lingering for a moment longer than she knew he should have.

All the feelings and emotions of the past weeks started to flood her. There were obvious physical effects that this man was starting to have on her. At that moment she wanted nothing more than to run for cover.

Aron broke the silence by asking, "How have you been feeling?"

It was a very simple and genuine question, and she knew that. She felt very shy all of a sudden. "I've been fine."

She could feel the now-familiar tension that had been surrounding them over the last week. Bringing them together seemed to amplify it exponentially.

"Sara, listen…I've come to tell you that I want to help you escape Valina."

"What?" she said more intensely and in a tone louder than she should have. She pulled herself together and continued in a loud whisper, "You can't be serious. If you were found out, you'd likely be killed!" It suddenly struck her that she had just put his safety above her own escape.

He immediately responded, "And you will most definitely be killed if you stay here. Vasin is still more determined than ever to find the book. In fact, he left the celebration tonight to investigate a potential lead on the book's location. Sara, once he finds the book your death will quickly follow."

Sara thought hard for a moment, knowing that the words he said were true, and that if she had any hope of escape left she would need his help. Her failed escape attempt was, if anything, proof of that. She trusted him now, and she knew if he said he'd help her, then he would. And while she was utterly confused about what her role really was or should be in this whole situation, she wasn't about to let anyone dictate her future, especially not her death.

A long silence ensued and was broken by Sara's one word: "When?"

"I don't know yet, but I'll come to you soon and let you know the details."

Vasin and one of his men stood in the library. Two guards stood watch just outside the doors. Vasin asked, "I thought you said you had some information on the whereabouts of Shalin?"

"Yes, we thought we did. We had been told that the woman Hecate had Shalin, but when we questioned her and searched her home, we found nothing. She denies any involvement."

Vasin felt extreme frustration. Why was he not able to make progress in finding the book? He did trust Hecate. If she said that she did not have it, then she did not. "Have you found out anything more regarding how Sara was able to travel from Earth to Esereth?"

"No. Nothing."

How was she able to do it? It was a mystery to him. He felt certain it could not have been Shalin; the book only allowed the people of Esereth to travel back and forth.

When Vasin had sent his men to Earth to capture Sara, the plan was to hold Sara until Kalen complied and provided him with Shalin. He had been angered when he found out that one of Kalen's men had interfered and aided in her escape; however, he had been shocked when he'd found out that she had somehow traveled to Esereth. It was a true sign. His father had told him about a prediction that Shalin had made regarding a *savior*—someone who would save Esereth. He'd had a revelation, and as such his plan had changed. Sara was not just a way to get Kalen to submit, she was a much bigger part of the solution. *She* was the one that Shalin spoke of.

∽

Kalen met his spy in the woods about one mile outside of Valina. It was dangerous, but necessary. "You saw her? How is she being treated?" Kalen asked the man.

"Yes, she's there and being treated well. Vasin's been letting her move freely within the city."

"You haven't made contact with her, have you?"

"No."

"Good. We can't risk it. If she knows we're coming it might put her in additional danger. When are you to watch along the wall?" Kalen inquired.

"I'm on watch for a week at a time alternating every other week."

"Where is she staying?"

"Vasin has her in a room on the far east side of the palace."

"OK, we're just about ready."

Kalen and the man parted ways in the dark of night, each heading back to his own temporary home. He had been relieved to hear that she seemed to be treated well. The rage he would have known if it had been anything different would have been too much. Vasin, his once beloved brother, had turned into a man he no longer knew. A man he could not trust.

THE DREAM

I have learned, that if one advances confidently
in the direction of his dreams, and endeavors to
live the life he has imagined, he will meet with
a success unexpected in common hours.
—Henry David Thoreau

Sara awakened in a cold sweat before dawn the next morning. The dream was back. And it was showing itself with an intensity like nothing she had ever felt. Not even the dreams of her father all those years held the same level of fervency.

"*Transitio in lucem. Salvum planetarum.*" The same words spoken in the garden of her dream—spoken from the book just before her travel here, but this time it was not just a dream. She could feel Shalin, which she kept at her side at all times, vibrating and humming those same unknown words. The movement of the book was similar but somehow different from just before her journey to Esereth from Earth.

She sat up in the bed in her room and pulled the book from inside her nightgown. It had an eerie, light-green glow and was still decidedly pulsing as if it were alive. There was no predicting when it would decide to act or come alive.

"Would it send me back to Earth?" she asked herself. "Wait," she suddenly shifted thoughts, remembering the contents of her dream.

At that moment she knew she needed to get down to the garden. She needed to bring the two pieces of her dream together. She didn't know why, but she trusted the book, and she believed that it was important to find out what it was trying to tell her. Sara, still in her short-sleeved sleeping gown, slipped on a light robe and her slippers and then slowly walked out the door of her room. She was hardly dressed for this, but she could not wait; she had to get to the garden immediately. She peeked around the corner of her door toward the hallway, and seeing that the coast was clear, she started to quickly tiptoe down the hall and toward the great staircase. Luckily for her, Vasin had stopped posting a guard at her bedroom door. It was likely all part of his logic that she had finally accepted her fate on Esereth.

Though her steps were light down the staircase, the sound coming from her slippers echoed across the large stone hall. This made her cringe. Her heartbeat picked up and her body doubled the speed with which she traversed the staircase and headed out the large wooden door that led to the garden. What she wouldn't give for a little carpet right now.

The morning chill hit her like a wall as she stepped over the threshold of the door and out into the garden. Sara involuntarily shuddered at this. For a moment she reconsidered her journey, but shrugged and silently acknowledged that she was undeniably too far into it to turn around and head back upstairs. She quickened her pace and headed to the spot in the garden where she'd been sitting in the dream. As she did so she could feel the bottoms of her slippers getting damp on the cold, wet ground.

This place was different. With dawn light not quite over the horizon, the garden took on an eerie glow, much as the book looked now. As she got to the center of the garden, the book started resonating with a light whistling sound. That, she hoped, meant that she was getting close. Close to what, who knew, but she was ready to find out. Then she noticed it— noticed that the large, old tree that was in the center of the garden was *not* in her dream. She had been sitting in a chair in its place. There must be some significance with the tree or the place that the tree resided. She walked over to the tree and touched its thick, majestic trunk, and the book immediately stopped its trembling. The glow was still there, but fading quickly, and the words she'd felt and heard earlier had stopped.

She felt extremely disappointed. She began to back away from the elderly tree in the hopes of restarting the book and in doing so backed right into a baffled Ifan.

"Ifan! You scared me."

Sara immediately slipped the dark and now quiet book back into the pocket of her nightgown and hoped that Ifan had not noticed it. Luckily for her, Ifan seemed not to as he was focused on other things...namely Sara's disheveled and somewhat indecent appearance. She must have looked a sight in her thin night robe and slippers.

Ifan was looking a little embarrassed and very confused. "Sara, what are you doing out here?"

"I, uh, don't know."

It was lame. She knew it. And as if to prove her correct, his left eyebrow lifted questioningly at her declaration. They both stood in silence for a moment; then Ifan seemed to decide that he would accept her lack of answers and instead shepherd her back to her room. He put some pressure on her elbow to guide her inside.

"It's absolutely freezing out here. You need to get inside immediately."

This was a more assertive side of Ifan that she had not seen yet. He was usually blushing horribly by now. Why was he not right now? She decided not to argue and conceded to herself that she would try to come back to the garden later tonight. She definitely could not attempt to bring the book out in the open with all of Valina up and about. She started a slow walk with Ifan to the doors of the palace. He took off his dark brown woolen coat and wrapped it around her. She'd started to protest but then thought better of it; she needed to avoid a scene and get upstairs as quickly as possible. She did not want to arouse suspicion about why she'd been up this early and out in the garden. She was very close to finding out what Shalin was trying to tell her. She knew that now. And it was something big. Big enough, she hoped, that it would answer many of the questions she'd wanted— no, needed—to have answered since having been hurled onto this planet.

Her thoughts were broken by another voice. "Sara, Ifan, what's wrong?"

Sara looked up to see Aron watching with concern, his eyes narrowing as he caught sight of Ifan's coat around her. Was that jealousy she saw in his face? Sara read his face and felt immediately as though she'd been convicted of a crime that she had not committed. And this made her mad.

"This is not what it looks like." She couldn't help herself from this need to defend herself in this situation.

"And what exactly is that?" Aron snapped. Ifan looked even more befuddled and made the mistake of trying to intercede in this dangerous conversation.

"Sara was out in the garden alone…"

Sara interrupted, "No, Ifan, it's OK. I couldn't sleep, and so I needed to get some air. Ifan ran into me and very logically pointed out that I should not be out at this hour."

Aron didn't look convinced, but beneath that she thought she saw concern. He said, "I agree with Ifan. Sara, you need to get back to your room. You shouldn't be out here alone."

She nodded in wholehearted agreement and without another word headed directly inside the glass doors and toward the staircase to her bedroom. She couldn't get away from that awkward situation fast enough.

Sara knew she had to get back to that garden and soon. There was something there related to the book and the secrets it held. She knew it with certainty. She couldn't go back to sleep after returning to her room. She sat, instead, on her bed propped up against the massive wooden headboard, her mind racing. After about an hour, she felt the sudden rush of adrenaline as she came up with a plan.

She did feel some level of guilt in dragging Balu into her scheme. There was risk in bringing the book out into the open in broad daylight, but she knew she was on to something important. And she also knew she couldn't do it alone; she needed some help.

She met Balu at the bottom of the stairs that morning. "Good morning, Balu. Will you come to the garden with me?"

They walked to the outer perimeter of the garden before Sara spoke again. "Balu, I need to ask you something."

"Sure, Sara."

"Do you trust me?"

"Yes."

"Are you willing to help me with something that Vasin might not like?"

His eyes turned into saucers, but that was the only indication that he was surprised by her question. He nodded slowly to answer her question.

She took a deep breath and slowly pulled the book from her dress pocket. "I have Shalin."

She thought that he might run away screaming, but he did not.

After a moment with his brows furled in deep thought, he said to her, "Yes, Sara. This is how it should be. You are the keeper of the book."

She felt him wise beyond his years with that statement, and she knew she had made the right decision. She trusted him, and his help was the only way she might figure out what secrets the great tree in the garden was holding.

"OK, here's my plan…"

They agreed to meet in two hours at the bottom of the stairs. There were several guards who were often in the garden, making it difficult to get close to the tree with the book without being seen. Balu would provide a distraction that would allow her to accomplish this.

Two hours later, Sara walked slowly down the stairs that were now so familiar. She'd memorized each step. She did not want to think about this place feeling a little like her new home, so she concentrated on her plan.

She spotted Balu at the bottom of the stairs, chatting with another man who lived in the castle. There was always something to do to keep the rooms clean and the food flowing, and there were a large number of workers who maintained the great estate. She could always tell those people because they all wore the same green tunics. Balu saw her coming and smiled at her. She tightened her grip on Shalin and felt ready for what she knew she soon might learn about the book.

They walked together toward the garden. There were two guards hovering around the center where the tree was located. The area around the tree reminded her of an exhibit at a museum: people could look, but they could not touch. It suddenly dawned on Sara that there was something important about the tree, but what was it?

Balu and Sara nodded at one another, and Balu walked up to the guards motioning them toward a bench some thirty feet away from the tree. They'd agreed he would fake an injury while playing near a small pond on the south side of the garden. Injuries were treated with very high priority, and it would likely take the guards several minutes to address the situation. They would know at that point that he had lied, but Balu had assured her that because he was a boy they would write it off as mischief.

As soon as the guards were out of the way, Sara walked with determination toward the massive and wise tree. Its lowest branches hung but a few feet above the ground. She knew there was something there, and she knew the tree was the key to getting out of this place and to finding out just what her role in this world was. Shalin dutifully started to vibrate once she reached the location, and she knew that she had found it. Sara stood next to the tree and leaned her head close, turning so that her ear was just a few inches from its trunk. At the same time she placed her hand on the rough bark. It seemed ridiculous, but she could almost hear the tree breathing as if it were human. It made her own breath catch, and she prayed that she would be able to find out the message it had for her.

She slowly pulled Shalin from her pocket and felt it pulling her toward the base of the tree. As she reached the ground next to it, she saw that the roots had created a small, open crevasse. The opening had been hidden under leaves and dead brush. Wedged in that hollow area was a ragged piece of parchment that looked very old. She barely had enough time to grab the small piece of paper before the guards realized that Balu was not hurt and that Sara was near the tree by herself. She stood up, shoved the parchment into her pocket along with the book, and tried to act normally.

One guard asked as he approached, "What are you doing over here?"

Sara replied, with as much confidence as she could muster, "I was just walking through the garden. I love to sit by this old tree."

The guard seemed satisfied with this and didn't really have any reason to question her further.

She took a deep breath, gave Balu a nod, and hurried back to her room.

౧ఞ

Sara sat on the floor, her back up against the side of the bed. She was focused entirely on one thing: the small scrap of paper clutched tightly in her hand. It was as if someone else had been holding it, and she was doomed only to look, unable to take action to find the answers she craved. She couldn't force herself to take the simple action of actually opening it.

"What is wrong with me?" she thought.

Her life had taken such an unexpected and extreme turn these last weeks she wasn't sure that she could ever get her past life back or go back to the way things were. And not even what was on that parchment could help her to do that. The realization that nothing could fix where she was right now in life was devastating. That naive hope she'd once felt of just forgetting everything was replaced with fear and the lack of courage to see what was next, to discern whether or not she might find the answers and her way back home to Earth, and to see how this would affect her newfound family.

It took an hour before she somehow found her way and her courage to look closer at the paper she had taken from the tree. In some ways, just finding the paper had helped her to gain a new relationship with both the present and the future. She no longer knew where she was going, but one thing she did know with her very essence was that she was being led by the book and this world. She was on a new quest now, to go where this world required her to go. She was a part of both Earth and Esereth, and they both needed her. They were calling her. Suddenly, she felt a moment of peace with the present. And because of this, she also felt calm about the potential future. Ready now, she slowly unfolded the wrinkled parchment. She was surprised by what it held.

It was a drawing with symbols running throughout. She'd seen some of Valina's written language, and this looked nothing like it. She couldn't decipher any of it, but she knew exactly whom she needed to talk to about this—Hecate. She was the only one who could help.

Sara decided after some deliberation to wait until nightfall before going to find Hecate. She could not let anyone know what she was doing. Only Hecate could know. There was something about the woman; her loyalties were the same as Sara's. They were to no one man, only to Esereth and Earth.

The hallway floor outside her room creaked in places as she walked, and she cringed at each of these spots, sure that someone would hear and she'd be shepherded back to her room. Or worse, they would see the precious cargo she had—Shalin and the parchment—but none of that happened. The guard at the front doors had his head bowed in a sleep deep enough that he was snoring. She picked up her pace and exited the palace, heading down a small alleyway that led to Hecate. Sara noted the silence while she walked. Without the hustle and bustle of the daytime activities, there was very little sound left. It was a city that was truly allowed to sleep. She felt very alone.

∽

Aron watched her leave the castle. He had been coming back to provide a report from a recent patrol. Seeing her sneak inconspicuously out the doors of the palace had surprised him. Aron followed her down the dark alleys of Valina. He had slowly been gaining on her and managed to silently and quickly sneak up behind her to grab her by the arm and whip her around to face him.

At first her eyes grew large with surprise and fear and then they narrowed with indignity. "What are you doing here?" she sharply whispered.

Aron responded more harshly then he meant to. "I could ask you the same thing." He was sorry that he'd made that remark. Now was not the time. He went on to say, "Sara, you have to stop doing this; it's too dangerous, and we are so close to being ready to try to leave Valina. You must do nothing risky until then."

Sara just as quickly replied, "It's important that I see Hecate—now."

Aron, who was getting more frustrated by the moment, replied, "Don't you understand that if Vasin finds out what you have, it's all over?"

"What do you mean?" she asked.

He sighed in frustration and then said, "I know that you have the book. I know that you have Shalin."

Sara looked shocked at first but then quickly regained her composure. She responded, "How?"

He said, "It's not important."

"Aron, why are you trying to help me? I don't understand. You could very easily bring us both back to Vasin."

Aron stuttered a little at this. "I—I—there's no time for this."

Sara managed to step forward so that she was just a few inches from Aron to look him directly in the eye and say, "You must trust me. I have talk to Hecate. She's the only one who can help me. She's the only one who can help all of us."

The resolve in her dark eyes was his undoing. The intensity he felt for her in that one moment was more than anything else he had experienced in his life. He pulled her to him and kissed her with all the emotion and passion that had been building since the day they had met. It seemed that he would follow her into the depths of hell if she had asked him to. She slowly moved away from him, looking up into his eyes. Neither saying a word they turned, hand in hand, toward Hecate's house.

⚮

As they approached Hecate's home, Sara could see smoke rising from the chimney and a dim light from that fire illuminating the windows. Someone must be there. Aron knocked lightly on the door and it seemed to hear them as it slowly opened on its own. Hecate was sitting in an old, squeaky, wooden rocking chair, head bowed as if she was concentrating on something very important.

Hecate slowly lifted her head and said with a seriousness that made them both tremble, "I knew you would come again…when the time was right."

Aron and Sara slowly crossed the threshold and walked across the room. Aron remained standing, but Sara sat down on a small stool that was next to Hecate.

Sara said, "Hecate, the book has been speaking to me."

"Well, what has it been saying?"

"*Transitio in lucem. Salvum planetarum,*" Sara repeated with a distinct certainty—it was emblazoned in her mind.

Hecate nodded knowingly. "It is a language that is as old as the cosmos itself. Your people on Earth know it as Latin."

This confirmed Sara's suspicions about its origin, as it had seemed familiar, but it didn't make sense. "I thought Latin originated on Earth in ancient Roman times. How is it probable that they could be the same?"

"People on Earth may have believed that it was their creation, but it was only *found* by humanity." Hecate grabbed Sara's hand and said, "The phrase is, '*Transition into the light. Save the planets.*'"

Sara cringed inwardly. All of this was leading her to a place that she was deathly afraid of dealing with. "Hecate, there is more." She pulled out the small slip of parchment from her pocket and handed it to the healer. Aron looked on curiously at what she had handed Hecate.

Hecate took a deep breath and said simply, "This, my children, is a map."

CHAPTER 10

THE MAP

The key to our universe is in each of us.

Hecate held in her hands the paper Sara had found. "Specifically, this is a map to find the key to Shalin, but you both should know that no one was ever meant to find the key—or the map."

Hecate paused for close to a minute before continuing. Neither Sara nor Aron said a word.

"Long ago, the ancestors of Esereth used the book to maintain harmony and order on Esereth, but for reasons no one knows, they hid the key, keeping the book forever closed. The only things left were the stories and knowledge passed on from one generation to the next. Secrets have surrounded Shalin for many generations. Aylmer, your grandfather, told Kalen and Vasin that if the life force on either planet were to be destroyed, the other would also see the same end; he was passing on the heritage of the book, but he could not have known that

Vasin would try to manipulate that fate instead of embracing it as his forefathers had done and as Kalen did."

Sara listened carefully but knew that she had no choice but to try to find the key. They must know what the truth of all this was—they must know what Shalin had to tell them.

"Sara, there is great danger in going to find the key," Hecate said. "There was a reason they hid it."

"I know," she responded.

Hecate sighed. "All action is motivated by one of two emotions—love or fear. Both are great forces, but they can create very different outcomes. Vasin, while his goal of saving Esereth is an admirable one, has chosen fear to drive his path, and because of it he is willing to do anything, even sacrifice you and the book. Sara, just be sure you understand what compels your decision."

"Hecate, I will find the key," Sara said firmly. "If I can open the book, then perhaps I can find the answers we need and keep peace on Esereth. It's our last chance."

Hecate nodded her head in agreement, then held the map in both hands in front of her face, looking at the scrolling more closely.

After studying for several minutes she said, "According to this map, you must travel through the Trab Woods to the Great River of Hafu. The key you look for is somewhere along that river. True answers you will find there, but I'm afraid it will come at a great cost to you, Sara."

Hecate's words weighed Sara down mentally as well as physically. She could almost feel her shoulders starting to droop as those words sank in. It took an extra bit of effort on her part to control herself and to stay focused on what must be done. Letting fear and emotions get in the way in a time like this would not help anyone. True heroes had the ability to control their emotions as well as actions in times of extreme pressure and chaos. She hoped desperately that she could be that person in the face of her own challenges.

"Sara," Hecate said, "Vasin believes that if he can sever the connection between our universes that our fates can also be separated. I am afraid he will set something completely different into motion if he is allowed to continue. He does not understand that we are all joined with one another and with everything in our universes. It's an illusion to think that we can ever by separated. Always remember that."

Sara knew the fate of both Esereth and Earth rested with her, and now she knew what she must accomplish.

∽

It was late. One of Vasin's men had abruptly awoken Balu and brought him from his room down to the great hall. The boy stood with his hands behind his back, staring at Vasin and looking extremely distressed.

"What happened in the garden earlier today, Balu?" Vasin asked.

"Nothing," Balu responded meekly.

"Now, I know that can't be true. The guard said you lied about having an injury. Why would you do that?"

Balu stood silent now, with eyes wide.

"I know you and Sara have grown quite close over the last several weeks—tell me."

Still silence.

"Balu." Vasin's voice hardened, and he switched tactics. "If you do not tell me what is going on, I will have to separate you from your brother and sister."

Balu looked up at Vasin, his bottom lip starting to tremble and face flush, he said, "Sara has the book."

"What book?" Vasin responded intently.

Balu whispered in shame, "Shalin." After saying those words Balu started to sob.

Vasin was shocked. Vasin couldn't believe that the book had been under his nose all this time. He had been waiting to kill Sara...waiting to make sure that he could get that book into his possession. Vasin knew that if he had both the book and Sara, his plans for saving the planets could be completed.

Balu asked, with tears in his eyes, "What are you going to do? Don't hurt her."

"It's none of your concern, Balu," he said sternly.

Balu, still obviously upset, ran from the great hall.

It was no longer of import to Vasin. He called over to three nearby guards, "Go and retrieve Sara—now."

The three men moved quickly, reaching Sara's room in just a few minutes. They did not knock, but instead barged right into the room. To their surprise, the room was dark and empty. One of the men walked across the room and opened the doors to the balcony. He looked out across the garden courtyard below. It was just as lifeless. He reentered Sara's room and said, "She's not here...now what?"

The other two men still stood at the entrance of the room. One of them replied, "Let's start sweeping the city. She couldn't have gone far."

∾

Sara and Aron left Hecate's home and began to walk toward the palace.

After a few moments, Sara spoke. "Aron, I must leave Valina. I have to find that key. It's the last chance we have to find answers."

"You're right that you must leave Valina, but you are *not* going alone. I'll go with you. I will help you find the key."

Sara shook her head and replied, "No, you can't. This is not your responsibility."

"That's where you are wrong, Sara. I've been waiting my whole life, knowing that there was something I was meant to do here, and this is it. I know it more clearly than I've ever known anything in my life."

Sara looked intensely into his eyes and saw that he was right. She did not respond to his statement but only nodded her head.

Aron continued, "We should leave tonight; it's sooner than I was planning, but the situation has changed, and to wait could put you in more danger. I know the guard who will be coming on duty just past midnight. He will help me."

Sara replied, "That's just two hours from now. We need to go back to the palace to get the supplies I've been gathering."

"Ok, but let's be quick. We haven't much time."

They traveled via the back alleyways toward the castle. Suddenly, Sara felt a chill and a shift in the wind. The hair on her arms stood up as if warning her of the danger that was about to befall both her and Aron.

Three men in palace garb appeared from inside a dark doorway just ahead of where they walked. They marched toward Sara and Aron, and one of the men wasted no time in grabbing Sara's arm and swinging her such that her back hit hard against the nearby stone building. That violent act caused the air in her lungs to be involuntarily pushed out of her. And when she subsequently tried to breathe in, an involuntary high-pitched sound occurred where there should have been air rushing in. It wasn't until her third attempt at a breath that she finally had some success.

Aron reacted to this with rage and lightning reflexes, unsheathing the weapon he had under his coat, but the other two men had the advantage over him. They were able to wrestle Aron to the ground and take his weapon.

Sara screamed, "Aron, no!"

The fear she felt was like cold, hard steel. The man covered her face with one hand and began roughly grabbing at her clothes.

"What do you want?" she attempted to say, but her communication was severely muffled by her assailant's hand. It was when the man stuck his hand in her pocket that she received her answer. He rifled around and then pulled out Shalin.

"Oh God, no," she thought, "not the book."

And though he now had the book, they were not through. Her aggressor said to her, "You are coming with us."

Sara started to protest, but then she turned her head to see that Aron had successfully been able to turn the tables and disable the other two men. He now moved to take out Sara's attacker. The last man, seeing this, let go of Sara abruptly and ran into the dark street. Without the force from him holding her, she slowly slid down the wall onto the ground and into a sitting position, knees bent to her chest.

Aron immediately ran over to her. It felt very quiet and surreal suddenly. Sara stared off into space. Aron grabbed her arms and pulled her up, shaking her just a little. He whispered harshly, "Sara, are you all right?

She said nothing. He shook her harder and said, "Are you OK?"

She had what felt like a few new bruises, but the only words she could think to mutter were, "Shalin... Shalin."

Aron knew immediately what she meant. Those had been Vasin's men, although he had not recognized them specifically.

They stood embracing for several minutes, neither speaking.

Out of nowhere, as if to give them both a message and some peace, it started to snow. The first snow of the season. Sara lifted her head from his chest to look up and observe some of the largest snowflakes she had ever seen. There was no wind; all had gotten eerily calm. The flakes meandered, taking their own sweet time getting to the ground. Any sound around them was muffled in the presence of the fall.

Aron let her go but kept her hand. That physical connection, while small, was the only thing that enabled her to stay standing. She couldn't believe that she had lost Shalin. She felt as though a piece of herself had been taken. Her attachment to that book had grown exponentially since her arrival on Esereth. She knew that for certain now. This sense of loss caused her to grip the map in her front pocket more tightly. They had been very lucky that the attackers hadn't been smart enough to take that, too. And because of that misstep, they still had a chance to save Esereth and Earth. She would not lose the map. She could not.

"Aron, we must still leave Valina tonight, especially now."

He nodded.

"And we still need the supplies," she added with the subtle implication of return to the palace.

Aron replied, "No, it's too dangerous now. Vasin will be waiting for you. I have a few supplies that I've already gathered that we can use."

"Aron, it won't be enough. We're going to be traveling alone in the winter wilderness for an indeterminate amount of time. Over the last weeks I've been putting together a pack of provisions for just this moment. I foolishly attempted to escape the last time without proper preparation; I will not make that mistake again."

She could see the conflict in his eyes. Finally, he grudgingly said, "All right, but we'll use a back entrance into the palace. We'll be less likely to be seen." It was a reluctant compromise. He knew the danger they were heading back into.

The entrance that Aron spoke of was toward the backside of the palace and accessed through a wooden door that was partially submerged below street level. It looked as though it hadn't been used in years. Aron tried to open it, but it wouldn't budge. It was jammed. Aron grabbed the wooden ring shaped handle, put his shoulder up against the door, and then forcibly pushed. After the third shove, the door gave way, causing him to stumble forward just a bit due to the built-up momentum.

He turned to her and whispered, "I'll wait here outside and keep watch. You go in and get your supplies. *Hurry.*" Surprising her, he leaned in and in one fluid motion he pulled her to him and kissed her on the lips. She felt breathless.

Sara walked through and saw that she was in one of the palace's many cellars. Wooden shelves on every side of her were layered with either food or barrels, likely filled with shal. She'd previously noted that the people of the city had borrowed the palace cellars to store their own items. The low temperature and steady humidity was of real benefit throughout the year.

She wasted no time. She walked up the cellar stairs and entered the kitchen. She was able to get quickly from there to the stairs and down the hall to her room. Once in her room, she slid under the bed and pulled out her duffel-like bag full of supplies. She confirmed also that her ring was still situated in the pocket of the bag. She didn't want to admit it, but she knew that the ring her mother had given her was part of the reason she had been so adamant about returning.

Everything came to an end, didn't it? Everything had a beginning, and everything had an end. This was normal. Why was she fighting it so much? The fact was, she was scared, very scared, but she knew at the core of her very self, her soul, that finding the answers in Shalin—whether it was to be the end of Earth or Esereth—was what she needed to do. She owed these answers to herself and her two worlds. Esereth was starting to become a part of her, as it was already a part of her father. That acknowledgment did provide her some solace.

She swung the duffel over her shoulder and swiftly walked toward the exit of her room.

Out of the corner of her eye, she caught the movement of a shadow next to her balcony door. That dark shift in light made her heart beat faster. Something wasn't right. Before she could get her fingers around the latch of the door, a familiar voice called to her from several steps behind.

"Sara."

She turned abruptly toward the voice and saw that it was her father.

CHAPTER 11

AN UNWILLING EXODUS

Sometimes we have to rescue
ourselves from ourselves.

Kalen had finished his plans for Sara's rescue. He had the execution of the events down to the minute. There was no room for error, as they had only this one attempt.

The plan was for Kalen's spy to be on watch at the wall tonight and to provide a signal when it was safe for the men to approach, but it was past time for the expected sign. Kalen was afraid something had gone wrong. He couldn't bear to lose her, not again. It had almost killed him when he'd had to leave both her and her mother back on Earth. It was a parent's worst nightmare, to lose a child. And he'd already missed out on so much of her life. Her transition from child to adult had seemed instantaneous, even though over twenty years had passed for her. Now more than ever he wanted to try to get those years back. He wanted to know his daughter again.

Kalen was suddenly alerted to the small blinking light from Valina's wall several hundred feet away. Relief washed over him. It was the signal. His man had come through. This guard was crucial to helping Kalen, Daric, and one other of his other men, Georg, to enter the city through an abandoned entrance on the far side of the city. Ironically Vasin and Kalen had played there as children and found the secret entrance. What was once an innocent exploration of two young boys was now a critical tool in saving his family. The still-heavy cloak of night would provide them the cover they needed to get in and out of the city. They would meet Kalen's remaining men back here at their temporary encampment after they had returned with Sara. Kalen had chosen carefully whom he would take with him into Valina. He knew Daric would do anything to keep Sara safe, and he needed someone with that loyalty. He also knew that he had been distraught since Sara's kidnapping. Daric blamed himself; he felt that he had not been there for her that night she was kidnapped. Kalen, too, had felt this same wave of guilt afterward, but he knew it wasn't true. This was Vasin's doing, and he alone should take the blame. Georg had immediately agreed when Kalen had asked him to accompany them on the escape attempt. He was a quiet but large and stocky man in his thirties. He had dark brown eyes and raven black hair. He was a soldier in every way and solid as an ox. But more than that, he was a man who had basic principles. Kalen had known him for several years before he had gone to Earth. Georg had always been quietly at his side. For a number of reasons he couldn't express in words, he completely trusted the man.

Immediately upon entering the city, Kalen realized how much this place was still his home. He'd grown up here, worked on these very streets with the people he'd come to love. It made his heart ache to know that he would have to come face-to-face with them in battle. He had seen conflict and fighting while on Earth, and it had sickened him. He still hoped with all his heart that it would not come to the full-blown violence of war here, but the people of Esereth were blind and naive. They had been sheltered from the potential atrocities of bloodshed. And because of that, Vasin would successfully lead them into the inevitable conflict that had been brewing for years now. Kalen feared that there was no turning back for anyone. It had also saddened and surprised him when only a handful of the city's people had left to follow him on his quest. Only the people in the small villages surrounding Valina had risen up to defend his cause. It was they who had shown the courage to think for themselves and not blindly follow Vasin.

As they continued toward the main square of Valina, they could smell the fireplace smoke of many of the homes, smoke from fires that had burned out hours ago and were now just hot embers. That was to be Esereth's fate if he did not stop Vasin soon— just remnant ashes from a long-ago-stoked fire. How had it come to this? How had they not been able to work out an agreement to solve Esereth and Earth's problems? He knew that Vasin had changed, and that he and his brother had taken different paths in life. That saddened him. Vasin's arrogance and willingness to do anything would bring their people and this planet to ruin. He would become the very thing that they said they would never be. No, he could not look back but only focus on this moment.

They knew exactly where Sara was being held. They only had to make their way past the guards keeping watch near the courtyard garden and ascend to her room. Again, Kalen's years of living in the city proved crucial to making this attempt successful. He was able to lead Georg and Daric through the dark winding corridors of the castle, expertly avoiding all of Vasin's men.

❧

Her father—he was here—in her room. Sara couldn't believe it. She'd all but given up any hope of a rescue. So how could he really be here? How had he made it to Valina?

The weeks of emotions she'd pushed deep within herself involuntarily and uncontrollably emerged all at once. The tears began to flow down her flushed cheeks; her breathing became uneven and harsh, the supply bag forgotten and at her feet. He had come to rescue her. On some level she knew her emotion was related to the proof that she had not been abandoned. Someone had cared enough for her to risk life and limb to save her. And of course, the rest of the emotion was for her own well-being and that she just might make it off this planet alive.

Her father gave her a strong hug, kissing her wet cheek. She could see he was choking back his own urge to shed tears.

He grabbed her arm and said, "We must go. There's no time. Daric and Georg are waiting for us just outside." He pointed toward her balcony.

This last statement triggered realization of the full implications of her father's rescue. She could not leave without Aron.

"Father, no, wait. I can't leave, not yet."

"What? What are you talking about? You must come now. We have very little time before Vasin realizes that we are here."

She started to pull her arm away from him and said, "No, I can't."

He grabbed Sara's arm and pulled her out onto the balcony. She struggled at first, but the thought of now putting her father in danger caused her to begin to comply. Kalen pushed her toward the edge of the balcony and quickly tied a rope around her waist. She looked below and saw that Daric was on the ground just below the balcony waiting. She met his eyes and immediately saw the intensity in them. She, however, only felt confused. So much had changed for her since the day she'd been kidnapped. Aron had happened to her. She looked back at her father. It was all so complicated. Once again she had not been completely honest with her father. She had not previously told him about Shalin; now, she had not told him about Aron or the key. It was all happening too fast, and right now she was afraid for Aron's safety. Her father would not understand their relationship. He would not understand why Aron was waiting for her outside the palace. She must keep Aron safe at all costs. She would have to leave him without saying good-bye. She felt as though her heart were being wrenched from her chest.

She was hoisted down from the balcony by a rope wrapped around her waist. Daric and another man, who must have been Georg, were waiting at the bottom to receive her; and while this should have brought her some comfort, instead as the rope inched her closer and closer to the garden grounds, she started to feel real anxiety. And not because of the danger that the escape provided, but at Daric's presence.

Once on the ground he immediately embraced her in a strong hug.

"Sara, I'm so glad you are safe. We feared the worst."

"I know. Yes, I'm safe." Their eyes met for a moment.

They wasted no time once Kalen reached the ground. Sara and her father were handed dark green capes similar to the ones Daric and Georg already wore. As they made their way stealthily across the dark garden square, the capes blended perfectly with their surroundings. They were invisible. She saw that they were headed toward the back portion of the green. It was a forgotten spot, thick and unkempt. In her entire time living in the castle she'd never seen anyone spend time in the area they were headed. Tramping through the thickest part of the brush along the castle wall that encircled the garden was not an easy task. It was overgrown, not manicured like the rest of the foliage. And as such, thistly vines were maliciously scratching her exposed skin. After everything she had been through, the scratches were nothing, but they added some sort of insult to injury that made her angry. Why were all these things happening to her? She was seeking answers to questions that she felt would never get answered. Not in this lifetime, anyway.

She initially missed the shabby, partially deteriorated wooden door that lay flush with the ground until her father, just a couple of feet ahead of her, bent over and removed the brush covering it. It looked like the cellar doors she'd seen on farms growing up. It looked old and weathered, and it, too, had been taken hostage by the natural environment, causing it to blend seamlessly with its surroundings. Georg opened the portal, the hinges holding it in place squeaking in disagreement as he did so. Sara was quickly ushered through first and descended what she thought must have been at least twenty feet of stairs. Once at the bottom she felt hard, packed dirt beneath her. It was so utterly devoid of light that she couldn't even see her hand, which she now held less than two inches from her face.

Daric came down just behind her. He had a torch ready and lit it once he reached the last step. That increase of light didn't do much, although it did allow Sara a marginally better view of her surroundings. They'd just entered an underground cave of sorts. The walls were mostly stone, and they only had a few wooden beams for structure. While some of the cave looked man-made, most of it seemed to be natural. There was a small stream heading in a direction deep in the tunnel. She wondered if this was somehow connected with the construction of the city aqueducts. Or maybe this place had been carved out by that very stream long before she or her father or even the city of Valina had been here. It looked as if no one had been down there in years—or hundreds of years. Cobwebs were everywhere, and any suggestions of construction looked rundown and as if they'd not been used in years. Probably the most important thing the torchlight provided was that it exposed the long, seemingly unending passageway ahead of them. To her disbelief, Sara then realized how they had done it—how they had rescued her. They had headed to the castle and across the city via this underground path.

They followed its path for fifteen or twenty minutes before she saw a crack of light in the distance. This light undoubtedly led to the surface and to their exit from the city. Where they emerged was also somewhat hidden from the naked eye. It was an alleyway near the city wall. It struck her that they were only almost free. There was one more crucial milestone—getting through the city wall.

∽

Close to fifteen minutes had gone by, and Sara had not returned.

"Something's wrong," Aron thought.

He entered quickly through the cellar, tracing the path that Sara had taken through the kitchen and up the stairs. He looked in the direction of the silent, empty hallway ahead of him. It was too quiet. The feeling of urgency overwhelmed him. He dashed down the hall and burst into Sara's bedroom. The space was dark and completely void of life. The bag of supplies she had spoken of was sitting abandoned on the floor next to the door.

Aron was completely blindsided. He ran through the open doors to the balcony and looked over the side toward the garden grounds. She had literally disappeared.

჻

Sara, Daric, Georg, and Kalen stood at the bottom of the tunnel stairs and looked up at the exit of the passageway.

"Everyone ready?" her father whispered.

There were nods, but no one spoke.

Kalen went first with the others in single file behind him up the stairs. He slowly opened the door and stuck his head above the surface to see if they could safely venture out. They had only to cross the nearby street to reach the outer wall and drawbridge to finish the last leg of their journey out of the city.

After his quick check, Kalen ducked back down. Sara could hear him curse under his breath. It was subtle, but she knew that it meant that something was wrong.

To Kalen's surprise the man who had infiltrated Valina and was posing as a guard to help them safely enter and exit the city was no longer at his post. In his place was a real guard from Valina. Weapon in hand and defending his station, he stood between them and their escape from Valina.

Kalen said, "Daric, you will take Sara out of the city. Georg and I will disable the guard." Kalen leaned into Daric and said, "You must get her out at all costs."

Daric only nodded, and Sara could hardly believe the plan.

"Father, no, you can't. We must all go together."

He responded, "We will be right behind you."

"Don't worry, Sara," added Daric.

"Easier said then done," she thought.

They all very quietly emerged from the passageway. They crouched low to the ground and moved quickly to a temporary refuge in the dark shadows next to a building along a narrow alleyway.

"OK, Georg, let's go," Kalen whispered roughly.

The two of them stealthily moved toward the unwitting man. They slid with a prowling sleekness like cats. All understood the seriousness of their situation—they had one shot to disarm—and if they failed there would be bloodshed, or worse, death.

Even though Kalen and Georg had the element of surprise on the sentry, the man looked brawny and well armed. They came up behind him, each man grabbing one of his arms. A struggle ensued.

The guard was strong, and while he wasn't able to reach his sword, he was able to gain access to a knife in his boot. He wielded it with expertise, and both Kalen and Georg were struggling to bring him down without sustaining their own life-threatening injuries. Suddenly, the guard yelled into the blackness, "Intruders!"

❧

As Sara watched she could see a change occurring—the situation was starting to become unmanageable. Their controlled and quiet escape was starting to unravel like a thread from a loosely knit sweater. And to further prove that point, she saw suddenly a dark shadow emerge from a ledge along the outer wall about five feet higher than the place where Kalen, Georg, and the guard were struggling. The form leaped jerkily onto Georg from behind and in that one swift movement also managed to stab him in the shoulder. With a surprised look, Georg turned, and with what was probably pure instinct, he was able to grab the knife from his attacker and retaliate by stabbing him twice in the chest. The dark form, smaller now, crumpled to the ground next to Georg. Sara squinted and looked harder to see the figure. That small form, that shadow, looked now like nothing more than...a boy.

Sara suddenly felt a growing knot of truth forming. "No," she thought, "it can't be."

She suppressed her feelings for just a moment with denial, hoping desperately that she was not right. She looked harder toward the small form and saw a glimpse of his face. And that glimpse, that shred of real truth, caused her to physically feel as though she herself had been stabbed in the chest. It was Balu.

Georg had not realized until too late that his attacker had been just a boy. But none of that mattered, the damage was done. Balu lay unmoving. Sara felt nausea quickly following visions not only of Balu but also of his little brother and sister. She tried with some difficulty to take large, deep breaths so that she might not lose it right there in the middle of all this chaos. The cold sweat that had formed on her brow in trying to keep this control made her shake severely. None of this got past Daric, and he looked at her with great concern as she was inwardly working through her sudden grief. He pulled her next to him, holding her so close that she could feel his warm breath on the back of her neck.

She tried to make sense of it all, but it was hard. Balu must have been sitting watch with the guard. She knew that Balu did often sit with the guards, sometimes even on the later shifts. He had told her once that he went there to watch for his father's return. It had been a place of refuge and comfort for Balu because he felt closer to his father.

The feeling of lost control was complete for Sara now—that sick appreciation of how quickly things could go from one reality to the next. How quickly her life could change forever in a heartbeat. Without another thought, she started to move, her intent to head to where Balu lay.

To her surprise, Daric grabbed her wrist and pulled her back, bringing them both down to the ground on their knees.

"Sara, *no,* you cannot!"

"I have to help him. He's in pain and alone."

"No." Daric didn't budge. It was a command.

"He's just a boy." Sara was sobbing now.

"You cannot. You will risk the lives of your father and Georg. The pieces have been put into motion."

"He will die if we don't help him."

Daric responded flatly, "All of this is much bigger than one boy."

She felt as if she were in a bad dream and was helpless to stop it. But in a dream there was hope that she could wake up. Sara knew she had no such possibility. She was furious with Daric.

"How could he?" she thought.

She watched with paralyzed rage and sadness as Balu lay bleeding on the ground, his still body—his short little life—potentially snuffed out by this fighting.

She hardly even noticed the guard that Georg had finally taken down. It was time to make their dash through the final gate and out of the city. With one quick fluid motion, Daric picked her up in his arms and ran with her toward her father and Georg and into the forest. Sara's tears blinded her vision and her mind. Her grief blinded her thoughts.

Was Balu OK? She couldn't believe that he was really dead. She would not believe it. Not that it wasn't possible, but her conscience was not ready to accept that her escape attempt could be the cause of it. That feeling of responsibility was almost too much to bear. Who would watch over the twins now? Balu was a victim of this entire situation. It didn't matter that he was from Valina, or that this city, along with Vasin, wanted her dead. How was it possible for one side to be right? Especially if it involved killing another. They were navigating through a world of gray. There was no black, no white. In seeing how Daric had responded to the boy, she both loved and hated him for it. She wasn't sure who was right anymore, or if any one person could be right. Truth was becoming more relative by the moment. And believing that one side was completely right and in sole possession of the truth felt dangerous and confusing. Yet, that was exactly what she was a part of, wasn't it?

༄

Aron had been standing at the far end of the city wall for the last hour looking for a sign of Sara. Dawn was just barely upon the city, and he hoped it was enough to see something, although he wasn't quite sure what. He was desperate to know what had happened. Surely she had not left by herself, but—no, he reminded himself, the bag of supplies had been left in her room. He had also confirmed that Vasin had not gotten to her first; a guard loyal to Aron had told him that Vasin was regrouping now that he had found the book. He assumed that Sara was within reach, and there was no immediate threat of her escaping Valina.

Something else had happened to Sara. He sighed heavily with fear and anxiety. Suddenly, he saw shadowy figures just outside the city wall. He rushed over to the edge of the wall to get a better look. It was difficult with the lack of light, but he could make out just enough to tell that the form was familiar. It was Sara. Somehow her father had made it to her. There was no other explanation. Aron desperately wanted to go after her, but he did not. He stood there unmoving. He had to stay. He had to figure out Vasin's next move. It was the only way to keep Sara safe moving forward. Vasin would not stop—especially not now.

❦

They all made it safely back to their camp outside of Valina. Luckily Georg only had a flesh wound, and they healed it quickly. Sara knew they wouldn't stay at the makeshift camp long. Within an hour, the group began to move south toward the larger, more permanent encampment at Antek. There Kalen's men and the tribes would align.

The next days were a blur for Sara. They rode and they slept, reaching the outskirts of Antek quickly. Sara had been close to Antek prior to her abduction by Aron, but never near enough that she could see it for its full worth. Nothing could have prepared her for the size of it. It was a veritable metropolis. It must have been at least ten times the size of Valina, although not as heavily protected. She'd been told that it was a gathering place of many different tribes and cities. It was a melting pot for many different people.

Less than a mile from the city there was a large outdoor complex. It was a makeshift military base where the men who were to fight Vasin had been eating, sleeping, and training. The complex itself was about ten thousand square feet and had a roof, but no walls. It looked a little like a park pavilion except it was much larger and without the concrete slab and picnic tables under the roof. Many of the people spent the majority of the day working on support tasks to keep the installation running. There was a group of the men who maintained the weapons, hunted, and organized the various military training events. They had a small handful of women gathering basic supplies from the city. The fact that there were women at all surprised Sara. To date it had seemed consistent that women were not involved in or supportive of the fighting. In that way, women still had more traditional roles. And it wasn't as if women were treated as second-class citizens or as less important. On the contrary, they were very much respected, from what she had observed in Valina; however, the women there did only seem to perform certain roles in the society. In the case of war, she supposed, it was the natural tendency—battle was physical and violent. Stereotypically, men seemed to be better wired to handle those types of situations. Women were the mothers and the nurturers. At that moment, her own mother flashed into her mind, along with a wave of emotion.

Sara saw her father working alongside the men to unload gear. She walked over to him, feeling the need to tell him of her mother's death. He needed to know. There were so few minutes to talk about these types of things.

"Father," she said simply.

"Sara," he said back.

She took a deep breath to steady herself. She wasn't quite sure how he would take the news. With the time differences between Earth and Esereth, it had only been a couple of years for him since he'd left.

"I wanted to tell you…about Mom."

Kalen did not speak but waited for her to continue.

"She died. She was sick." Sara started to choke up at those words, and her father embraced her as the tears begin to flow from his own eyes as well.

She pulled back a little to face him, but his arms were still around her shoulders. "She told me to tell you that she loved you," Sara managed to say. "She knew, didn't she, that you were still alive?"

"Yes. She knew who I was and where I came from."

This both saddened Sara and made her feel happy—a confusing mix of emotions.

"Sara, your mother would have been happy to know that we found each other."

She nodded in wholehearted agreement, tears streaming down her cheeks.

⁓

It had been one full week since the escape, and Daric could not stay away from Sara anymore. He knew that she had not approved of his actions and words during their escape from Valina, and later he had found out that that boy she had tried to save had died. He felt sadness for her, but he knew he had done the right thing. It was very simple really. Sara must live. Kalen must live. There might be many a sacrifice along the way, but Daric was willing to do whatever was required to keep those things a reality.

He'd watched her, for the last hour, sit with several other men on a rounded bench that formed a semicircle. They'd just finished eating dinner there, and a boy was gathering the empty bowls from the stew in a container for washing.

The sun had gone down, and the chill in the air had a bite to it that made even him shiver. He walked over to her with a blanket and silently put it around her shoulders.

Daric looked at Sara and said, "We need to talk about what happened."

She replied softly, "There's nothing to say."

"Sara, I know you don't understand why I held you back from helping Balu, but know that it was the right thing to do."

There was silence. He could feel her straining to maintain her tense and immovable stance. He put his hands on her shoulders and raised her to a standing position. He then embraced her. She started to sob, her resolve now broken, and returned his embrace. She needed to connect with someone. She needed someone with whom to share her grief.

CHAPTER 12

VASIN'S ATTACK

It is well that war is so terrible,
or we should grow too fond of it.
—Robert E. Lee

Completely gone was the confident and wise leader Aron had once known—replaced, instead, with a fearful and obsessed man who had forgotten all else but finding Sara. Since her disappearance from Valina, Vasin could talk of nothing else but severing the link between Earth and Esereth—and Sara's death. Aron watched Vasin as he paced the main hall of the castle in Valina.

"I know that Kalen has taken her. We must attack them. We must retrieve Sara. She must be sacrificed or Esereth will perish."

Aron responded boldly, "We don't know for certain that Kalen has taken Sara back. And even if he had, we don't know where they have gone."

But of course, Aron did know that it had been Kalen. And he was reasonably sure where they had gone, but his allegiance had fully changed now. He would do whatever it took to keep Sara safe. That included watching over Vasin.

"Tell me again, Aron, why you were with Sara the night that the book was retrieved from her." Vasin eyed him suspiciously.

"I was escorting her back to the castle," Aron replied. It was mostly the truth. The men who had attacked him had told Vasin of his defense of Sara. This had put him in a very vulnerable position with Vasin.

"It was dark, and it was unclear who the men were who had attacked us. I did not know that Sara had the book, nor that you had sent the men to retrieve them. Vasin, we were physically attacked. I would have thought you'd have been glad that I defended her!" Those last words were emphasized and annoyed.

"Yes, I suppose you are right." Vasin sighed with resignation. This finally seemed to convince him of Aron's supposed and continued loyalty. Aron took a deep breath of his own.

"Aron, you can go now." Vasin turned away from him and walked toward a large map that lay across the table. With finality he said, "I have work to do."

The next day in a dark, forgotten room of the castle, Vasin waited. It was over an hour before the dark room was momentarily transformed with blinding light. Four men appeared out of the brief light carrying with them two large wooden crates, each holding up an end. The men strained with the weight of each box but managed in a controlled manner to slowly set the crates onto the ground.

"Did you get it all?" asked Vasin.

"Yes," replied one of the men.

"Good." Vasin smiled knowing that he now had what he needed to get Sara back.

Drizzle fell upon the camp near Antek. It was probably no more than a few degrees above freezing outside, and as such, it was the worst combination of cold and wet. Sara stood under a small lean-to where she was able to stay relatively dry. She watched some men nearby as they practiced sword fighting. They were in the open, and their clothes were visibly wet. While their tunics were water resistant, they were not completely waterproof. They seemed to hardly notice, though; the physical exercise generated the heat they needed to stay warm.

Vasin's threats and recent attacks had consolidated the tribes more than ever. New men were arriving to join the fight, and with them they brought supplies and swords. Sara's father never said it out loud, but she knew they were planning an attack on Valina and on Vasin. The evidence was all around her.

Daric came up next to her under the shelter and said, "Would you like to learn how?"

"To do what?" she asked blankly.

"To handle a sword."

"Me? Well, yes, I guess I would," she responded, a little surprised by the offer.

"I could teach you."

"I would like that." She felt shy when she said it.

"Come over, and I will give you your first lesson." He picked up a sword sitting nearby on the ground.

She stood up and walked with him over to an empty area several feet away from where the men sparred. He held out the sword to her and said, "Take it."

She attempted to comply, but was immediately surprised at how heavy the weapon was. She had to use all of her strength just to hold it up straight.

He responded to her struggle. "We will get you a lighter one, but this will work for what we do today."

He walked behind her and put his arms around her to help hold up the sword. She could feel his breath on her hair.

"One of the first things to learn is how to hold the sword." He helped her to properly clasp her hands around the grip of the sword.

Once satisfied he continued, "The second is stance. Your left foot will be back. Your right foot will be in front, facing straight ahead. Most of the weight is on the back leg. It is important that your front foot be balanced. This allows you to move quickly."

Sara nodded, understanding.

Daric was teaching her to take back some control of her life. It was working. She was starting to feel some simple solace.

A few days later, Daric approached Sara's encampment. Hers was a small tent on the very outskirts of the larger encampment. Daric had originally objected to the location, which added unnecessary danger to Sara, but she had insisted and in the end won. The camp itself was simple but adequate. It was well insulated and the bed was comfortable. It had all the amenities needed for, well, surviving.

Daric paused in front of the hut, stopping just short of the entrance. He didn't want to push her. He really didn't, but at the same time he needed to know that she was doing better. He needed to know that she was becoming whole again and would be OK. All of these things, he knew, were more selfish than selfless of him, but he needed them as much as the air he breathed.

"Daric, hello," Sara said softly from behind him before he'd actually had a chance to move past his thoughts.

Daric jumped, turned toward her, and then laughed at himself. "I didn't know you weren't inside. I...I just wanted to see if you needed help with anything."

"Come for a walk with me?" she asked avoiding his question.

Without saying a word, he took her hand and led them into the nearby forest.

They walked slowly with eyes focused on the forest floor. The ground was thick with brown now, and the brittle leaves made a crunching sound with every step they took. These were the last remnants of fall. Winter was upon them.

After several minutes of walking, the forest opened up to a lake that was about half a mile in circumference. The wind drove uniform-patterned waves across the pure, dark-blue water. It was clear that the source of the lake came from the nearby mountains.

Daric stopped several feet in front of the shoreline, turned so that they were facing one another, and grabbed both of her hands. He broke the silence by saying, "Sara, we need to talk."

She looked up at him but said nothing.

"Please let me help you to move on...to heal." And with that statement, he pulled her closer to him.

Daric cared for her and wanted more from her than just friendship, and he knew that her feelings for him were strong, but something was holding her back.

"Daric, I can't." She turned her head away from him.

Her plea fell on deaf ears. He sighed with a mix of frustration and tenderness and finished the action he had started. He took her lips captive. She allowed it but did not respond in the way that he had hoped. Daric could not himself change the way he felt. It was too late for him, too late for his heart. She pulled away from the kiss, though his arms still embraced her.

"Daric this can't work—it just can't."

He'd not been able to think about anything or anyone but Sara over these last weeks. And there it was, in these woods, her rejection of him.

"Why not?" he asked with a subtle level of irritability.

"Daric, I...I care for you greatly, but there is someone else."

He nodded in acknowledgment of her crushing words. "Who is it? Someone on Earth?" he wondered jealously.

There was nothing more to say. He broke their embrace. They turned back toward the encampment leaving the cold, crisp simplicity of the lake behind them.

∾

As Sara and Daric reentered the main camp, they heard men yelling, and they could see a crowd centered around something. Sara and Daric ran toward the direction of the commotion. Now closer, she could see a dark-haired man in Valina garb of green and gold lying next to a riderless horse. He was beaten and bloodied, and his clothes were torn. One man bent over him and began to prop him up with his arm around the back of the wounded man's neck. Sara's father was not far behind and was almost to the wounded man's side. She could see that he was coming back into consciousness, but just barely. He was mumbling something. It was hard to hear. Sara leaned in farther. The hurt man's mumbling surprisingly became words that Sara could understand.

The man said, "Vasin, he…he has brought back a weapon from Earth."

His father asked, "How do you know this?"

"I saw his men return from Earth with it."

"What kind of a weapon?" her father asked.

"It's what the people on Earth call a *bomb*."

Sara pushed past her father and the other men and knelt next to the afflicted. "What kind of a bomb?" Oh no. There would be no coming back from this. If these people changed from swords to bombs, it would be all over. She prayed that it was not some sort of chemical or nuclear weapon.

The man did not speak another word. His eyes fluttered for a moment and then closed. She looked at her father with a horror that matched the message of the newly deceased. She couldn't stop the tears that started to run down her face.

Sara resolved in that horrible moment that this man's death would not be in vain. "Father, I need to show you something." He somehow seemed to understand the relative importance of what she needed to tell him. He gestured for her to follow him.

Sara now stood before her father just inside the entrance of his tent. She took a deep breath and fumbled briefly with the folds of her dress. She pulled the parchment from a pocket in her dress and held it up to her father.

"What is that?" her father asked.

"Hecate says it's a map to find the key to Shalin. Father, if we can find the key, then perhaps we can find the answers we need to stop the war."

He eyes widened, but he shook his head. "No, Sara. The ancestors hid the key for a reason. They separated it from the book to keep us safe. We cannot assume that we know better than they did."

"Father, it's the only way."

"No, we have to meet Vasin head on. As long as you are safe he cannot win. We must hurry, though. Time is of the essence."

Sara did not agree with her father's decision, but she trusted him. Ultimately, she felt as though she had no other choice but to comply.

The encampment spent the majority of the next morning preparing for the dead man's funeral. She was told that it would take place at a death marker. It happened to be the same one Sara had seen just outside Antek several weeks ago.

They traveled on horseback. The weather continued to be cold and dreary, making the few miles they journeyed seem endless. The ceremony for the man had a pronounced intensity. They stood around his body, which was perched on a hill of cut branches—basically firewood. She'd read about cultures that burned their dead, but she'd never witnessed it. She most certainly had no idea how the event might make her feel. A man spoke words she did not understand, but knew them, based on Hecate's previous information, to be Latin. "*Corpus ad Esereth...spiritus ad unam vitam.*"

Her father stood beside her. He told her, "The ceremony for this man does not reject, but embraces the brevity of life. It calls for us to accept the present moment and not to live in the past or the future. It asks us to help send the man's physical life form back to Esereth and celebrate that the man's spirit has gone back to the larger life force that is present across all of the universes."

After the fire was lit, they did not wait, but mounted their horses and began a very slow march back toward the encampment. It was odd, but she truly felt closure for the man. The event made her feel more a part of this world than ever. She desperately wished she'd been able to have this feeling at her mother's funeral. It, in contrast, had given her no peace. She'd only felt pain and loss.

She entered her tent that night feeling especially exhausted. She lay down able to quickly drift into a dreamless sleep.

ॐ

Sara awoke to the sound of a loud, high-pitched whistling sound. It was just a precursor to another more intense, low-pitched rumbling sound that occurred just a couple of seconds later. Her physical response to these sounds was immediate. Her heart was beating rapidly in her chest, and she shot up vertically, quickly swinging her legs over the side of the bed and planting her feet firmly onto the floor.

"Is it an explosion?" she asked herself. The sick feeling in her gut told her yes.

Adrenaline started to take over. She grabbed her sword, which was just a couple of feet from her on top of a small chest at the foot of her bed. Thanks to Daric and her recent lessons she felt comfortable enough with it that she believed she might actually be able to inflict some damage.

Her sleeping gown she converted into a shirt, although too thin for this winter-like weather. She threw on the pants that she had commandeered from her father and attempted to walk toward the opening of her tent. It was dark, and she was not quite awake, so she tripped, just catching herself, over the chair by her bed. At the tent flap she pulled on her boots, which were waiting for her. Her hands were shaking out of control. Her body was telling her that something very bad was happening. The shaking caused her to take a few extra seconds to get her boots on, and she cursed her clumsiness.

As she stepped out of the tent and into the outside world, she could see bright flashes of light in the distance. The contrast of these flashes with the night were blinding and had her seeing spots as she tried to refocus on the path ahead of her. The dread and confusion, accompanied by a strong wave of fear that came over her, were hard to stifle. It was the same type of feeling that had occurred on the night she had been kidnapped by Aron from her father's camp. Except this time it wasn't swords. This time Vasin must be attacking with the bomb. It had to be. It was the only thing that explained what she was seeing. Everything she'd been afraid of was now coming true.

This must be how her ancestors fighting in wars must have felt. It was a surreal feeling. It was as if someone else were really going through this situation and she were only the observer. But she knew that she was not the observer and that she must do something—and fast. She looked around, waiting for something that would tell her where to go or what to do. But nothing did, so she did the only thing she could think of. She started to run toward her father's and Daric's tents. She'd not gotten more than several feet from her tent when the dark image of a man approached. For a moment she hoped it might be Daric, but that feeling vanished when she saw the flash of steel coming toward her. Instinct took over. She dodged the attempted blow and raised her own sword in response, swinging at the man but unfortunately missing. What little confidence she had vanished as she reaffirmed in her head that she had no chance against a man twice her size and strength.

Fate decided to intervene. The ground shook around her from a nearby explosion, and the man lost his footing while she was able to keep her own. It provided her with the moment of advantage she needed to inflict a blow. She didn't waste any time and was able to injure the man in the chest. The emotional response she felt at hurting another human immediately and acutely washed over her. Adrenaline was the only thing that kept her from being completely paralyzed by what she had just done. She dropped her sword and ran. She had no idea if she had killed the man or not, but it didn't matter. She had crossed a line tonight, regardless of whether it was in her own defense. These thoughts made her nauseated, and she had no choice but to stop running, put her hands on her knees, and bow her head down. She took several deep breaths, holding each one in longer than the next. Was she hyperventilating? She raised her head to see that one of those bright, blinding lights that had been in the distance was suddenly upon her. She had no more time to think, just run.

Suddenly, there was another explosion, this one much closer.

Her last memory was being thrown through the air from the force of the blast—then blackness.

∾

Every bone in her body ached. She tried to focus on her grandmother's home, peaceful sounds of singing birds and crickets in the evening, and long walks in the woods. It was almost enough. These pleasant thoughts were invaded by more painful physical realities. She opened her eyes to see blood puddled on the ground next to her. There was so much of it.

She could hardly move. What was wrong with her? She felt as if the weight of death was upon her. And ironically enough, there was some truth to that statement. She could see now that there was a man lying on top of her. With the closeness, she could see his face and on it the now familiar look of death. The sudden wave of claustrophobia associated with that realization astounded her. She felt nothing more now than the immediate need to be free of this lifeless body. As if in answer to her prayers, she suddenly felt herself being lifted up—almost floating in the wind like a leaf in this autumn trend. But she knew that she wasn't a leaf, and she wasn't floating. She squeezed her eyes shut, hoping that perhaps the motion would stop, but unfortunately the only thing that succeeded in doing was making her queasy. Was it possible to feel that nausea if she wasn't really moving? Maybe this was from her wounds.

She didn't have the courage to open her eyes to find out until she heard the sounds of a familiar, low voice: "Sara, look at me."

"It can't be," she thought. Aron? Was it really Aron? Or had she truly lost it?

"Are you OK?" the voice asked.

She finally opened her eyes. The blackness turned into blurry light, and then the blur started to take the form of an angel. Then the angel turned into the concerned face of Aron.

"Aron" was all she could mutter. She attempted to say more, but her body, battered and bruised, was stubborn, and only an additional small grunt and a small smile upon her lips would it allow.

With his arm under her head and a hand lightly stroking her cheek, he said, "Sara, you're going to be all right. I've got you now."

A voice suddenly interrupted them. "Let her go!"

It was Daric. Sara, a little more coherent now, felt the shock of having the two of them together and in the same place—with her.

All in one fluid motion, Aron moved away from Sara and unsheathed his sword.

Aron said, "You don't understand what you're doing. I'm not going to hurt her."

"I understand everything I need to. I know who you are, *Aron*. Step away from her, or I will kill you."

Sara painfully propped herself up on one elbow and interjected weakly, "Daric, it's OK."

He wasn't even looking at her, because the conversation had ended, and they were running toward one another in mortal combat. They both were strong and expert swordsmen. The fight was immediately difficult and ugly with neither man gaining much ground in the next several minutes. Additional explosions surrounded them. The chaos made this personal conflict even more complicated.

Abruptly, the fight stopped. It was inadvertently interrupted by several of Vasin's own men. They attacked Daric, allowing Aron the critical time he needed to pick up Sara and take her to his horse.

"Daric," Sara muttered as they moved away from the fighting. She slipped in and out of consciousness over the next several hours. The wound on her head made her feel nauseated for the short periods of time she was awake. And she was tired—so very tired. Despite the fatigue and pain she felt, she needed to know what had happened to the camp—what had happened to Daric and her father.

She forced herself to ask, "Aron, where are we? And what happened?"

"Right now we're about ten miles from your encampment, or at least what's left of it."

She responded quietly and with difficulty, "The attack—the explosions—it was Vasin?"

She knew the answer. It was Vasin. He had struck back, and hard.

"Not again, please no more death because of me," she thought. Her vision started to blur. That was all the energy she had for now. Aron tightened his hold on her as they continued to ride onward.

She awoke feeling much better the next day. Aron sat next to her, both of them now on the ground. Every time she awakened, he was next to her. He never left her side. He gave her water to sip and continued tending to her wounds with all the healing power Esereth had to offer. She was doing much better, and the healing liquid worked fast. It was an amazing thing about this world. They really had surpassed anything on Earth. And it was all so natural and a part of the connection that they had to their world.

She still had so many questions. "Tell me what happened. Where's my father?"

Aron look at her, sighed, then replied as he redressed the wound on her head, "It was Vasin. He attacked your father's camp. There were severe casualties. I don't know what happened to your father."

"And what about Daric?" she asked, wishing she didn't need to. "Is he OK?"

In response to her question she saw his jaw set and his fist clenched, turning his knuckles white. "I didn't kill Daric, if that's what you are asking."

Sara was at least somewhat relieved by that ambiguous response. She cared about Daric.

He continued, "I honestly don't know if he's OK or not. Vasin is growing more powerful by the minute. Since he retrieved the book, he's been acting crazy. He feels as though it is Shalin's will."

"Aron, I can't believe that Vasin would use the weapons of Earth."

"Yes, I truly never thought he would go that far."

Sara realized at that moment that Aron was alone in all of this. She said, "You've left Vasin—does he know where you are?"

Aron said, "I'm sure he knows now, but it no longer matters what he thinks. Sara, I'm here for you. And I'm here to ensure that you get what you need to do what's right for our two planets. I just wish I'd been able to warn your father before the strike. Not even I knew what he was planning until the men were on their way. Vasin trusts no one now."

"We did know that there was a weapon," Sara said. "We got word from one of my father's men who had been inside Valina...but we weren't ready to attack yet, to stop him, and so he got to us first."

Aron nodded gravely.

They traveled northwest at an excruciatingly slow pace during the next day on horseback. It was all that Sara could manage. Aron continued to tend to her wounds one at a time over the next day so that she was now almost fully recovered. Sara was conscious most of the time—still weak, but alert, and she very quickly regained her strength.

It was early evening just past sunset. On this cold, hard evening they'd not said much to each other. Sara was sitting next to the fire, and Aron was unpacking their gear and making camp for the night. She looked over at Aron. He moved across the camp in fluid motions, his muscles flexing with every movement. He was powerful. He'd been working the better part of the evening to set up camp and ensure they were properly protected for the night. Despite the frigid temperature, he only wore a thin shirt and trousers. He'd shed his tunic hours before, and small beads of sweat were starting to form on his temples. How much had he risked by rescuing her? She would probably never fully comprehend the sacrifice he had made: abandoning his home, his beliefs...and all for her. How could she really understand any of that? She'd never had to leave her family for another…not yet, anyway.

"Aron, please come over by the fire and sit…just for a while," she requested.

He stopped, put down the saddle he'd been moving, and walked over to her. He sat very close to her, but not touching. It didn't matter that there was no physical touch; the electricity of every moment now between them was flowing and continuous.

Sara unexpectedly asked Aron, "How do the healing vials work? Your ability to heal is amazing, you know. There's nothing like it on Earth."

"Actually," he responded, "there is something like it, but the people of Earth are just not as tapped into it."

"How is that exactly?"

"Well, your medical science can explain physical responses involved in, say, healing a cut: your body first controls the bleeding, then stops infection, and then rebuilds the tissue. But what science doesn't understand is how the body knows to do this; it doesn't know what force, what intelligence, powers this healing process."

Sara listened intently.

Aron continued, "The healing ability in the vials just amplifies the force that your body is already able to initiate."

"I see," she said, nodding. She really did see. It made sense. "You know, I wounded—maybe even killed—a man that night of the attack...I didn't want to." This was an abrupt switch in topics, but she couldn't help herself. The need to discuss what she had done had been waiting just below the surface.

"I know you didn't," he responded.

She understood the full devastation of that attack. It was not just in lives lost. It was much more than that. It was the first real act of war, of large, full-scale group aggression, on Esereth. And it was a huge blow to the strength of her father's cause. No one could fully defend against Vasin now. The tribes had been broken apart, and the few survivors likely went back to their own people. The destruction, fear, and pain caused by this attack had sent the people of Esereth down a new path. She just hoped it was not too late to save them all—from themselves. Fear had spun things into full motion.

She didn't want to deal with the realities that lay beyond this forest. Why couldn't they just stay here alone, living in peace? Why couldn't they just ignore the other insanities going on around them? She also couldn't stop dwelling on her recent insecurities. How did Aron feel about her? Did he love her? He was so hard to read sometimes. She knew he cared. His actions told her that much without a doubt, but she could not distinguish between his loyalty to her cause and his love for her as a person.

She sighed and said, "Aron, what are we going to do?"

He turned toward her and touched her face. "We'll figure this out."

At that moment, he closed the distance, cupped her face between his hands, and began to kiss her. They melted toward the ground with Aron now on top of her. His hands started to move from her face to her waist, but then he stopped. Sara stilled, too. She was very aware of the sudden change between them. His face was still so close to hers, and she could feel his warm breath on her. It made her own breath catch.

"Sara, do you love Daric?" he asked.

The question caught her completely off guard—and for a moment she didn't answer. This pause made him frown.

Finally, she answered him. "I care for him deeply." It was an honest answer.

His eyes darkened, but he did not move. He did not speak.

She looked up at him and whispered with such raw emotion that it made her shake, "Aron, I love you. I've never felt this way about anyone."

In response to this, he pulled her closer, and the kiss that followed represented the pureness of that truth. The electricity was undeniable. The kiss turned explosive. She knew, now, how inadequate words were to describe what she was feeling for him, and she desperately wanted Aron to know what she was feeling. This physical intimacy and its connection allowed transcendence of the normal verbal boundaries, but it, too, had barriers. They had a spiritual connection that not even the physical could properly communicate.

Aron broke away and whispered harshly, "I love you, Sara."

Later that night, as they lay next to one another, Sara felt that the moment could not have been more perfect. She closed her own eyes and focused on this moment. *There is only ever this moment. Life is always now.* She could no longer hear anything around her—the night, the sounds of the woods, the crackle of the fire. She could only hear Aron—hear his breathing—could only hear his earlier words to her: "I love you."

And as if he had had heard her thoughts in his sleep, he pulled her even closer to him and brushed his lips against hers. Her whole body responded to this, and so did his.

CHAPTER 13

THE QUEST FOR THE KEY

*Hope is the thing with feathers That perches
in the soul, And sings the tune—without
the words, And never stops at all.*
—Emily Dickinson

The next morning Sara awoke still tightly enfolded in Aron's arms. The cool, damp morning air made her involuntarily shudder, and Aron responded to this by drawing her in closer. She knew with all her soul that this felt right. That he was right. And that her purpose in this life was right. Her true path was right.

She felt the gray space she'd been struggling with fall away. She saw the glimpse of black and white she needed, the sense of purpose and a clear path ahead of her.

She did not want to leave their small cocoon of safety, warmth, and security, and face the challenges and the insanity of the world around them, but they arose, grudgingly, out of their slumber just after the sunrise. Sara suddenly felt alone. Being away from Aron for even the moments it took to gather their food and supplies and pack up camp so that they could move on for the day was almost too much to bear.

The small fire that Aron had built out of dry brush was just large enough to provide her a bit of warmth against the cool, brisk morning. She stretched her hands, palms away from her and toward the flames. She watched her fingers and held them to the fire until she could barely stand the heat. The smoke from the fire wafted occasionally back in Sara's direction, burning her eyes just a bit. The heat and the pain were worth it. They helped her to focus on the physical moment and not on her emotions.

There was a drink warming on a rock next to the fire. Sara moved over to pick up her mug and sipped twice, feeling the warm liquid flow down her throat.

"Aron, do we know how far until we reach the destination on the map?" She pulled out the worn parchment from her pocket and held it out toward him. Aron, several feet away, finished loading the horses.

"I've been taking us toward the Hafu River. This is what Hecate described in the map. It's hard to say, though, how close we are." He shifted topics. "The horses are ready to go now."

The horses—she inwardly cringed. She'd already been struggling with the short distances they'd been traveling, but she knew they would have to pick up speed and travel longer if they were going to find the key in enough time. She had problems riding on a good day, let alone after the ordeal she had just been through. From what she could tell on the map, they would likely be traveling for a week or more on horseback, but this was purely a guess. The map was anything but precise, and she was afraid that she was grossly misjudging distances and travel times.

Little did they know that their travel on horseback would be shorter than she initially thought. It was after only three days of riding that they found themselves staring at a crossing for a very large river. Or rather, more accurately, a raging set of rapids. This milestone was both encouraging and daunting. Based on their discussions with Hecate, this had to be the Hafu River. Sara felt certain that they were on the right track, but the small stream on the map was nothing like the raging waters that stood before them. The steep, jagged edges of rocks that interlaced the width of the river were treacherous. Sara had done some white water rafting as a teenager, but that was nothing compared to this. She doubted the best of rafters could navigate it, let alone a novice like herself.

Based on the map, they would need to turn and follow the path along the Hafu River. And that would be easy enough, except that the path they would have to follow was extremely rocky in places, and dangerous. Even if they made it themselves, there was no way they could take the horses. There was no room for them to navigate.

Aron stared at that river for a long time and then turned to her and said, "We have to use the river. We have to travel down the river via boat."

She whispered raggedly, "But how? It's much too dangerous, and I hate to state the obvious," she gave him a sideways glance, "but we have no boat."

He responded, "We'll build it. It should only take a couple of days. We'll move much too slowly by foot. Traveling via raft will cut our travel time by at least half. We have no choice. And it's likely these rapids won't go more than half a mile or so—they typically don't last long distances. If we can get through them, then we can easily finish the trip down the river to our destination." The response was a logical one, albeit aggressive.

Sara nodded but could feel her stomach starting to ache and palms starting to sweat with fear of what they were about to do. And due to the time they needed to build the boat, she would have a couple more days to feed her fear. Dealing with time was something she had never been good at. Instead of time making things better, it usually managed to either get her madder or to thoroughly psych her out. Time and her mind had been enemies in the past, but she must do better this time. On some twisted level she thought, "What's the worst that could happen—death?" The pure and simple fact that they were all headed to that same place at some point in this life somehow brought her both the peace and courage for what she must do.

That day they spent several hours just walking along the riverbank to find a spot benign enough so that, once they'd built the raft, they could launch it into the river. At first Sara was certain this place didn't exist, but luckily Aron spotted a small embankment that just might work.

After the second full day of construction, she marveled at what they had accomplished. She was no boatbuilder, but this raft looked as if it just might work. This boat of theirs was a very simple, sound design, and in cases like this, simple was the requirement. Aron told her that he had made several that were similar to this in his youth.

Luckily they had with them most of the tools required to cut down the nearby smaller tree limbs. They'd pulled it all together with a combination of some makeshift ties from their supply bags and a natural glue that Aron had concocted from the surrounding forest. The cement-like substance came from a combination of the sap from nearby trees and a powder extracted from a small brown root prevalent in the area. It was unbelievable to her how combined, these two natural—and unto themselves benign—things could create something so strong.

It was a flat structure, with the logs in line, one next to the other. It was large enough, just barely, to fit Sara, Aron, and their gear. There was a vertical pole that they fitted in the middle to anchor their supplies. Since they would no longer have their horses to do that piece of the heavy lifting, it was yet another reason that they needed the boat. Traveling on foot with supplies for any period of time was almost impossible.

༄

On the morning of their third day on the embankment, Aron was finishing loading the raft with supplies, and Sara brought the horses to a nearby grassy spot. Reluctantly, she left them there and watched them as they grazed, oblivious to their abandonment. She walked back toward the river thinking about the upcoming dangers and the fears she would soon have to face. She was so thankful that she'd had someone to go through all this with. Aron gave her strength, and the bond that they had forged was getting stronger each day. She couldn't imagine her life now without him.

Sara climbed onto the now ready craft, and sat squarely in the middle just in front of the supplies and food. Aron then pushed the craft from the sand embankment into the shallow river water's edge, wading knee deep before jumping on himself and sitting directly in front of Sara. This gave the raft enough momentum to catch the flow of the river and upcoming rapids. They had about thirty feet ahead of them once they were in the middle of the river before they reached the first set of rapids. They had tied rope onto the raft in several places so that they might have something to hold on to as they maneuvered their way through the perilous rapids. She had wrapped the ropes several times around her wrists so that she had a good hold on the raft, but also not so tight that, if the raft flipped, she couldn't still free herself and try to swim away. Aron used the ropes as a foothold, keeping his hands free to use the makeshift oar he had fashioned from one of the branches.

"Well," Aron said matter-of-factly, "I guess we're as ready as we're going to get."

Sara gave only a nod as her response.

And with that ceremonious beginning they approached the first set of rapids. The watercraft started to bob wildly, but miraculously everything stayed intact. This prompted Aron to give, to himself mostly, a small grunt of pride for the proven quality of his workmanship. Additionally, their gear had not yet shifted noticeably and was so far handling the stresses well. She was very thankful that Aron had been able to expertly tie down the supplies so that, short of someone cutting them loose, they were a permanent part of the raft.

The water was now crashing around them, much of it splashing both her and Aron. The water was very, very cold, likely only a few degrees above freezing. Within a couple of minutes they were both soaked and frigid. This feeling of raw cold and wet brought back unwelcome memories of her recent, previous escape attempt—the cold, dark waters of the moat around Valina—and unguarded emotion from that near-death experience. It made her feel the need to gasp for air even though she was nowhere close to drowning…yet.

"Get it together," she admonished herself.

She must focus on the critical task at hand. It was crucial that she not be distracted for even a moment. It could be the difference between life and death. They were now getting ready to go through about a ten-foot drop. Two large boulders were on either side at the end of the downward slope. They had to maneuver directly between those rocks or be crushed. Aron's muffled words were telling her something important, she knew, though she could not decipher a single word with the screaming waters around them. He might as well have whispered to her. She tightened her grip on the ropes, almost cutting all circulation in her wrists. If that was what it took, then so be it. She moved back a couple of inches so that she sat with her back flat against the pole. She hoped that might help to stabilize her position on the raft. They started to drop, and for a couple of seconds it felt surreally as though they were flying. But then that feeling transitioned into a perception of *crashing*. In that moment she started to scream. She realized that she was not just releasing the fear from the current moment but also the frustration from the last weeks.

They hit hard at the bottom of the mini-waterfall and slapped the water with extreme force. Aron was now rapidly rowing to maneuver them between the two rocks. It was working. His muscles tensed, but he never wavered, and in fact the raft was making quick progress to be in a good position. Sara watched as they floated through the chasm between the boulders. He had done it.

The river began to calm, and Sara could see ahead of them that the rapids were coming to an end. They had successfully made it through the first set of them. Somehow they had really done it, and they were still in one piece. Aron turned around and looked at Sara. He wore the biggest smile she'd ever seen. She couldn't help but smile widely back. Then the smiles turned broader until both eventually broke down into hysterical laughter. Soaking wet, tired, and cold, they hugged one another, relieved. Sara started to believe that maybe they could do this. Maybe they could get down the river and actually find the key.

❦

They had been three days on the river. The map had not been clear how far downriver the key might located. Additionally, the key, the river, and an unknown symbol all came together at a point on a map. Sara and Aron weren't even entirely sure whether they had missed whatever that symbol was, along with the key, some miles back. They stopped only in the evenings to make camp along the embankment. Their initial elation at having mastered the river was now replaced with frustration and fear that they might never find what they were looking for.

On the fourth day down the river, they could hear a low rumbling sound. There was something odd about the sound. As they continued down the river, the low rumbling started to rise into something more. It sounded almost like thunder crashing.

"Aron, what is that?"

Aron paused unsure at first; then his eyes widened with a knowing look. "It's a waterfall," he said.

As they got closer to the falls, the water picked up speed and turned more rapid-like. Aron estimated that the waterfall was still some distance ahead of them, but both agreed that they did not want to risk heading through the unstable water or misjudging distance to the fall's edge. The time lost would be minimal at this point.

As Sara stared at the map, she realized the identity of the unknown symbol. "Aron, the symbol on the map...it's a waterfall," she said with sudden emotion.

He leaned over her shoulder to look and then nodded his head in agreement. They were close.

Despite keeping an aggressive pace, it still took them a few hours to reach the falls. The sound that had started as a low rumbling was now deafening. Sara thought the rapids had been loud, but they were nothing compared to this. The raw power of nature never ceased to amaze her.

As they stepped closer to the edge of the cliff to get a better view, she could feel on her face the mist rising up from the falling water. The base of the falls must have been at least a couple of hundred feet directly beneath them.

She looked at Aron and said, "Just how are we supposed to get down there?"

Aron had been thinking the same thing, she knew. He'd also been looking for a way down. "We'll have to leave our gear here. It's just us the rest of the way."

Sara felt as if this trip has been slowly stripping her of everything she'd ever known—both physically and mentally. She was way past feeling vulnerable, and she didn't like it one bit.

The roar of the falls made it difficult to hear, and Aron had to strain his voice to say, "We can use the rope in our gear; we have to climb down." That statement, though muffled, immediately caught her attention.

"Oh no," she replied. She'd never done anything like that before, and certainly now was not the time to start. She had barely been able to maintain her strength over the weariness she'd been feeling with the travel. Now she would have to be on the top of her game to survive rappelling down a cliff. She'd had enough misadventures as of late; this was not on her list.

She said, "I can't."

"What?"

"I can't do it. I just can't," she responded.

"Yes, you can, Sara. I know you can. We're close... close to what you've been searching for. Find the extra strength you need. Dig in and know that you can do this. You must do this."

She took a deep breath, knowing that he was right. Sara didn't know where exactly she would find that strength, but she knew deep down that she didn't have a choice. There were bigger things at stake here...much bigger than just her.

၆၅

Aron wrapped the thick, braided rope around a nearby tree stump. The spot looked as though it had been hit by lightning some years before, with only the base of the tree withstanding nature's harsh hand. He then tied a lasso-like knot at the other end so that they could use it as a foothold. They didn't have enough rope to get all of the way down to the ground, so they'd have to stop midway. Luckily there was a ledge about halfway down that might work. It was risky, but it looked as though, once they landed, they could traverse the length of the ledge to a rocky ramp and work their way down the rest of the way to the base of the falls. The ledge itself was thin. They would have to be shoulder to shoulder, side by side, the whole way across. And on their way down the rope, they'd have to land directly on target—there was no room for error or else they'd miss the small shelf completely.

As Sara began the slow descent, her fingers strained to hold the thick, rough rope. The pure force with which she held it started to scrape her skin and was getting more and more uncomfortable. But there was no way she was loosening her grip—absolutely no way. She could feel the sweat starting to bead on her forehead and under her shirt.

"Don't look down," she told herself sternly. "Stay focused. It's not much farther now."

Aron lowered the rope steadily the entire way, and she trusted that stability implicitly. Suddenly, she felt with her feet the firm, stone ledge beneath her. She had made it. She stood waiting as Aron expertly followed her down. It looked effortless for him, and for that she was glad. One less thing, or person, to worry about. He reached the ledge in half the time it had taken her. They had really made it! They held hands next to one another for a moment, neither saying anything, just soaking in the moment of closeness and the intensity of their situation. Aron pulled her to him, then slid his hand around her waist. They would need to make a small jump from the ledge to the edge of the falls, where the rocky slope was located, where that sharp decline should eventually lead to the base of the falls and onto the bank of the river below. They were able to transition from the ledge to the slope with relative ease, and they continued the more benign descent toward the bottom.

About halfway down the slope, Sara felt a soundless voice calling to her. She jerked her head in the direction of the falls next to them. She didn't know what she was looking for but continued to squint in the general direction of the falls, feeling as though she had to find the source of whatever was beckoning her. It was then that she saw a dark void behind the rushing water of the falls.

Sara yelled, straining her voice over the loudness of the falls, "Aron, I think we need to head that direction."

"What? Sara, what are you talking about?"

"I can't explain it," she replied, "but we need to head this way."

He didn't argue or respond further. He just followed her lead back up the slope a few steps to the edge of the falls and into the dark abyss just behind. It wasn't until she'd entered it that she realized they were now behind the waterfall and inside a cave. As their eyes adjusted to the small sliver of light coming through the falls, they could see that it was a vast, open space. It was also quieter there, the cave walls providing some amount of muffling of the waterfall just beyond them. The space looked as if it had been etched over thousands of years. It was too perfect to be anything other than a creation of nature.

Sara let the moment and her intuition guide her now. Aron seemed to know that he, too, should trust her. He pulled two large torches from their sole remaining piece of gear, the backpack he had shimmied down with. It was enough, along with the little light coming from outside, to provide an adequate view of their surroundings. They could now see drawings and script on the cave walls—pictures that, unlike this cavern, were definitely man-made. They scanned as far up as the light would let them see, at least twenty feet high. Some were as small as Sara's hand, while others were as tall as she was. She didn't know in what time or by whom the drawings had been made, and she was certain she'd probably never know. Aron didn't know either, but he instinctively moved closer to Sara and put one arm around her shoulder.

"Aron, can you read the writing?" Sara asked.

"Yes, some if it," he replied.

That was good news, as it might help them better understand. Together they turned their attention to the spot where the pictures and ancient writing began.

"Might as well start at the beginning," Sara thought.

The paintings on the walls showed two stories in parallel to one another moving left to right with one just above the other on the wall. The first scene, on top, began with a group of people standing on a green-and-blue circle, and the second scene below was similar, with a group of people standing on another similar green-and-blue circle. Connecting the circles and the stories were two bright green lines.

Sara spoke out loud, suddenly knowing. "Aron, are the circles Earth and Esereth?"

He nodded. "Yes." He pointed to the writing beside the pictures that proved it.

Sara spoke excitedly. "We're so close! I know it."

His eyes widened as he further read the text. "And, Sara, the two lines are two bridges between the planets."

She responded, "There used to be two bridges between Earth and Esereth?"

He nodded.

Sara continued her thought out loud. "Do you think that the people of Earth could once travel to Esereth just as you all do today?"

"Yes, that has to be what it's showing us."

Aron positioned the light so that they could continue reading the full story. They slowly moved from scene to scene, having to walk along the wall as they did. They began with the story on the top. There were two groups of people now instead of one. One group held up a book above them. The other group held a key. They were facing away from one another as if to show the separation of the key and the book. She saw that the book had the same ornate decorations as Shalin; this confirmed without a doubt that it was Shalin and the people of Esereth that she saw in this story. She was witnessing the disunion of the key and book.

In the final scene, only the group with the key was present, and its members were carrying the key toward a familiar drawing. It was the same as the symbol for the waterfall in their map. She could feel her pulse starting to quicken with the realization that the key might really be here in this cave.

She pointed to the bottom story now. "Aron, if the top circle was Esereth, then this bottom circle must be Earth."

"These people on Earth are shown still together in one group, not split," said Aron.

Sara continued, "But they also had a book and a key similar to ours."

In the next scene of Earth, a man was shown placing the key into the book. In the subsequent scenes they could see him rising with the book and key into the air toward a bright green circle of light. In the final scene, the man was gone, the light was gone, and the bridge from Earth to Esereth was gone.

This scene troubled Sara.

The paintings ended, bringing them to the entrance of a one-room cavern. The ceiling was at least fifty feet high. They'd reached the end of the cave.

Suddenly, Sara grabbed Aron by the arm and said, "Aron, look over here."

They could see a small golden glimmer of light in the middle of the cavern floor. It was reflecting the torches they had lit. Aron rushed over and saw that something was actually flush with the floor. There was a drawing of a man and a woman, one on each side of the engraved object. Aron's hand fanned over the source of the reflection and realized that it wasn't a picture but actually something that had been placed in the floor of the cave. Aron and Sara slowly carved away at the dirt with their fingers to reveal a box. It must have been very old, barely still intact, and about the size of a cigar box. After about fifteen minutes, they were able to extract the golden box from its resting place and easily open it. Inside was a small golden key with the same decorations as Shalin etched into its body.

"Aron! I can't believe we found it!" Sara was elated.

She reached out her hand and touched the key, still in the box, with her forefinger. It responded by starting to glow green just as Shalin had. The glow was reflected in Sara's face. She looked up at Aron, neither saying a word. The key then started to vibrate.

Suddenly, the cave, as if an extension of the key, began to shake as well. It was as if to cry out that Aron and Sara should not have been there or accomplished what they had. Dirt and stone started to vibrate, and now rocks the size of her fist were actively starting to fall on and all around them. Sara and Aron looked at one another with disbelief. Sara just stood there unmoving, feeling as if her limbs were frozen in place.

Aron, luckily, felt no such paralysis. He grabbed her arm and yelled, "Sara, come on!"

He pulled her in front of him, and they both started at a dead run back toward the entrance and the ledge where they had entered the cave. The shaking was becoming more intense now. The walls were actively starting to collapse, and the stones falling were as big as her head in some places. The thought entered her mind that if they didn't hurry, they might actually be buried within the falls. Sara kept a strong grip on the box and the key, and despite the exhaustion of her body, she managed to muster a final surge of adrenaline and use it to attempt to keep herself alive. It worked. She emerged into the light just outside the cavern. She turned around, expecting Aron to be right behind her, but instead he was nowhere to be found.

Without another thought, she turned around and headed back into the collapsing structure. She would not leave him.

He was lying on the ground just several feet away from the exit. He had a large gash on his forehead.

"No!"

She ran over to him, no longer concerned about the falling rocks and dust from the continued destruction of the cavern around her. She knelt next to him and put one hand on his head and with the other shook him.

"Aron!"

Amazingly, this seemed to rouse him out of his disoriented malaise. "Sara?" he said.

"Get up!" she screamed. "Get up!"

She draped his arm over her shoulder and between her strength and his they ran toward the entrance. Then he was able to gather his remaining strength and wits. He grabbed her around the waist and jumped for both of them from the cave exit to the nearby slope. It was not a moment too soon. The cave opening behind them collapsed completely, spewing bits of dust and rubble. Both were breathing heavily, hearts pounding. The only thing Sara could think about was that she still had the key. At all costs, this was likely the only way to save Esereth.

They slowly traversed the rest of the way to the bottom of the falls and to a grassy bank where they could continue more easily on foot. Once they reached safety, they stopped and sat for a moment, staring down at the box sitting on the cold hard ground between them. Sara's hands were shaking wildly. Aron grabbed them in his own to steady them and then pulled her toward him into an embrace.

"It's all right," he said.

She did not look at him.

He repeated more firmly, pulling her head up to look into her eyes, "It is all right."

That evening at camp, Sara lay on her back watching the night sky, the stars all around her. They seemed brighter than any back on Earth, and they also seemed to twinkle more. She looked for constellations similar to ones she saw from Earth. At first she thought there were none, but then she noticed something that looked akin to the Big Dipper. How could it be? She wondered how all of this worked between the two universes. Some things were most definitely different—but many were identical. Sara turned her head toward the two moons. She noted that one was significantly larger than the other, but both looked similar to Earth's moon's surface—gray, desolate, and devoid of life. Perhaps if she stared hard enough at the familiar sights they might provide her the answers she needed.

"No," she sighed, "nothing."

Since they had left the waterfall, she had been obsessing about what they had seen on the cave walls. Time had allowed things to sink in. There had once been a bridge from Earth to Esereth. This had surprised both her and Aron. Her mind could not stop the flood of questions that had surrounded the story of Earth. Who had the man been on Earth? Where had he, the key, and the book gone? If she put the key into Shalin, would that happen to her as well? And would the bridge from Esereth to Earth be destroyed, too?

She thought about Vasin. He believed that he could separate Esereth from Earth. Those drawings certainly seemed to support that possibility. It struck her that this struggle here—between believing that they were all a part of the same cosmic cloth and believing that they could be separated—was the same as on Earth. Many people treated others as though they were separate entities. It was the only way to explain how some people on Earth could do the horrible things that they did to one another. It was the only way to explain war. This feeling of separation also had led to a growing disrespect for all life on Earth, whether it was for plants or animals or the ground people walked on. Sara had, unconsciously, always believed that they were all connected. Now, consciously, she knew it.

◦∿

They agreed, in the morning, to head toward Antek to look for her father as well as any followers loyal to him. Aron did not know that Sara had another plan. She'd been over it in her head a dozen times, and a dozen times she had talked herself out of it. But in the end she knew she must go. And she knew that if she told him what she was planning, he would immediately reject it. She knew he would not understand it when he found out tomorrow morning that she had left to return to Valina without him.

That night, Sara walked over to the blanket they had retrieved from their sparse gear. It lay there patiently waiting to be lain upon and seemed to welcome her. She curled up onto her side and closed her heavy eyes. A few minutes later, she could feel Aron quietly lie down behind her in a spooning fashion and place his muscular arm around her waist. He pulled her in as close to him as was physically possible. It felt as though she could never get close enough to him. She took a deep breath to take in the familiar scent of him and stifled the urge to talk. He felt her breathe in, but he did not say a word, and she appreciated that. Instead he nuzzled his face into the back of her neck, causing her to give a small, involuntary sigh. He put his hand under her shirt, lightly stroking her stomach. He began to give small kisses to her neck, and she felt herself melt. She needed him to survive.

CHAPTER 14

FINAL JOURNEY

*One's first step in wisdom is to
question everything—and one's last
is to come to terms with everything.*
—*Georg Christoph Lichtenberg*

The next morning the ground hung heavy with dew, and the air smelled like a mixture of forest green and the charred wood from last night's fire. It was quiet and still dark, save a small glow of pre-dawn light. If felt as if they were the only beings in the world. Sara looked down at Aron still sleeping, and tried to memorize every last line on his face—the position of his body, his hands. Those hands were safe and strong. She loved his hands. She grabbed her small bag of food and supplies and tiptoed off into the forest.

༄

Aron awoke to find that he was alone. He felt an immediate jolt of fear. He looked around the vicinity of the camp—no one.

"Sara?"

No response.

"Sara!" He yelled it louder this time—nothing.

His fear suddenly turned to rage when he saw that her gear and portion of the food was missing. She had left him again.

Where had she gone? His mind raced. To Antek? None of this made sense. Why would she leave?

Then, suddenly, he knew. Deep down he'd somehow known that she would try to go back. But he'd been in denial...until this moment. Valina. She was headed back to Valina.

❦

The harsh reality of trying to go back alone to Valina very quickly settled upon Sara.

She sat on the forest floor, getting ready to sleep for the night. She'd traveled all day on foot farther downstream of the river, with no real idea of where she was headed. It was just past dusk, and she had built a very small fire, just enough for warmth. She'd brought only a small knapsack full of food and one blanket, and now she was certain she'd gone insane.

She thought about her decision. What was she doing? She'd barely made it to the falls with Aron's help, and the help of the river. How was she going to make it back by herself?

With a sigh, she sat down and pulled out the box with the key. This was the reason she had left. She knew that she had to return to Valina. It was like heading back to the lion's den, but getting that book back was the only way to gain the leverage she needed to stop Vasin. She would go straight to Hecate's, as the old healer was likely her only chance of figuring out a plan that might actually work.

She thought again of Aron. He would be safe.

She also knew he would not understand her need to go back to Valina and retrieve the book. He would only see danger for her and his need to protect her from it.

The weight of these worlds was on her shoulders and hers alone whether she liked it or not. She had not asked for this, but it was hers nonetheless. She took a long, deep breath, hoping to take in what strength she needed to find the answers and the path that she must take to save both Earth and Esereth.

She opened the box and looked at the key. It seemed to look back at her. She slowly picked up the key and held it up closer to her face so that she could look at the carvings. They were intricate and very old. Both Shalin and the key seemed to exude wisdom. They had withstood the test of time and had led the people on both Earth and Esereth. "Although, in humanity's smugness, they believed that they led and controlled *them*," Sara thought. It was a little too ironic. Perception of control was a dangerous and often misjudged thing.

Suddenly, she heard a rustling several feet away in the forest. She sat up, tense; her head turned in the direction of the sound. She tried hard to suppress a yelp of fear. She then watched as Aron came through dark expanse, stomping through the knee-high forest brush toward her.

Sara tersely said, "You scared me!"

"Me? You left!" He closed the distance between them and now stood over her.

Her shoulders slumped as she realized that she had truly messed up. "I'm sorry. I know."

"Why did you leave?" His tone communicated that he was very upset.

"Aron, I felt like I had to go…to keep you safe… and also because you wouldn't have let me go if you knew where I was really headed.

"I do know where you're headed—Valina."

This surprised her. "OK, and would you have let me go?"

He paused for a moment before speaking. "No."

She shook her head.

"Sara, we're in this together. I love you. We will get through this together. I will support you, even if it is to Valina."

She walked over and embraced him.

He spoke in a whisper into her hair, "So no more running off…please?"

She nodded and agreed, now truly believing that she would not, and that they would face what lay ahead together.

৵৶

Almost a week later, as they approached the massive stone walls of Valina, Sara contemplated how long ago it seemed since she'd arrived here the first time. It was all very deja vu. The first time, Aron had been her enemy. That first time she'd been scared and naive about the world—the worlds—around her. It all seemed to have happened to someone else a lifetime ago.

With the critical knowledge of the passageways at their disposal and Aron's knowledge of the watchtower layout, they were able reenter the city walls with relative ease. Sara was thankful for that bit of experience and knowledge despite its cost. She and Aron emerged from the underground passageway onto the street—at first, she thought unnoticed, but then she saw a man in palace garb standing several feet away from them. The look on his face began as surprise, but then morphed quickly to recognition. Before Sara and Aron could even react, he turned abruptly and ran in the direction of the castle.

They didn't have much time now.

They picked up their pace and headed straight for Hecate's home.

An hour later Sara and Aron sat in Hecate's hut listening with somber and somewhat saddened hearts.

"Sara, you are the real key. You are the one to save us all. The ancients knew that one day you would come. You would arrive in a time when both planets needed your help. The book is not good or evil, and for Esereth it has been a source of knowledge and peace because of how the ancient ones chose to use it."

These words caused a painful chill to slide across Sara's shoulders and down her back. Not because this surprised her, but because she now really began to understand and believe what her purpose in this life was. It was death.

At that moment, it became clear to her that while Vasin and her father truly believed that they were doing the right thing, they had both gone too far. This transition to violence, the attack on her father's camp, and Balu's death were all leading them further down the path of fear and violence. A path that the people of Esereth had, for thousands of years, *chosen* not to embrace. Nothing could justify these acts. It might very well be that it was time for Esereth and Earth to die or be destroyed by humans, but it did not change the fact that individuals still had choices.

Hecate responded to her thoughts. "Do not be afraid, Sara."

Their conversation was cut short as they heard the rumbling of men marching not too far outside Hecate's door.

"You both need to leave now—get away."

Hecate turned to a small, dark shape in the corner of the room. Until that moment Sara had not noticed that there was anyone else in the room with them.

"My granddaughter, Cerina, will show you a way out the back to avoid Vasin's guards."

The tiny girl slowly walked out of shadow and into view. It couldn't be, but it was. It was the girl who had given Sara the book back on Earth.

Sara gasped and said, surprised, "You!"

All the different pieces were starting to come together. Things were starting to come full circle. Hecate had known all along and had been involved in bringing Sara here. Sara knew that she should have felt betrayed at that moment for all the pain and suffering that had been brought to her since obtaining the book. But she did not feel these things; there was only understanding. Hecate had known all along that Sara must come here to fulfill her true destiny.

Following Hecate's granddaughter, Aron and Sara quickly headed out the back of the hut. After they stepped out the back, there was a commotion. Ten of Vasin's guards emerged from the darkness. They immediately grabbed all three of them.

Sara blurted out, "Stop!" This caused the men to take pause for just the instant needed for her to continue her statement. "I will show you where Shalin's key is if you let them go."

Aron yelled, "No, Sara, don't!"

The men ignored Aron. Instead they released both Aron and Cerina.

Aron said with a determined look, "Sara, I won't leave you."

"You have to."

One of the guards turned to Sara and said, "Give me the key."

She put her hand into her dress pocket and pulled out the golden key. They all were visibly affected by its appearance. They gathered their wits after a few moments, and the one who had spoken to her took the key from her hand and put it into his own pocket.

The guards walked away toward the palace with Sara, leaving Aron to watch, helpless with fear and anger.

༄

The guards opened the cell door in the palace and pushed Sara into the room. The shove was so hard that she could not stop herself from falling onto her knees with the palms of her hands flat on the cold, dirty stone floor. She raised her head, hands still on the ground, to look around. She felt as if she was reliving the same experience again, but with eyes more wide open this time. She started to pull herself up off the floor but stopped suddenly at a low muffled sound from the back of the cell. It ended as quickly as it started, just a small noise that could have very easily been missed if it had not already been so deathly quiet. Was she now imagining things, or was someone or something with her in this abysmal place? It was difficult to see almost anything in the cell with night now upon them.

Suddenly, as if to confirm that she was not indeed conjuring things, there was a slow shuffling sound. It was growing louder now and approaching her. Her immediate reaction was a strong wave of fear. This place and her recent experiences had done nothing to make her expect the best of a situation. How would she defend herself?

Before she'd even had the opportunity to physically react, she felt two strong, gentle hands around her shoulders raising her up from the floor. And then one of those hands slowly raised her chin up so she was looking into a pair of blue eyes. She sucked in a sharp breath and felt her eyes start to well up with tears—not from fear, but from a sense of pure relief. It was Daric.

"How did...?"

Sara didn't get to finish her question because Daric crushed her with a strong embrace and whispered, "Are you all right?"

She answered his question with a simple yes.

"Sara, I feared the worst, and we'd heard rumors that you were captured and perhaps even already killed by Vasin."

He sighed loudly and took her hand, leading her over to a small stone bench pushed up against the cell wall.

"Your father and I were among a small group of survivors from Vasin's attack on our camp," he said, now answering what had been her initial question.

"So, my father is still alive? Please tell me he is alive," she pleaded. She didn't think she could bear any other response.

He unconsciously ran his hand through his hair then said, "I don't know. We were separated after the attack. I only know that he was alive when I last saw him."

This small bit information at least gave her hope that her father was well.

Later that night she lay shivering. The cell was not heated, and the evening was frigid. Daric must have noticed this and without asking he moved from the floor to the cot where she lay. He positioned himself behind her and wrapped his arms around her shoulders. He was like an oven, and she was thankful for the comfort and closeness. Nothing had changed how she felt about Aron…or Daric. Daric was a good, caring man. She could not deny that she did care very much for him. She also knew how difficult it must be for him right now. She desperately hoped that he would not try to do anything more as they lay together. She felt vulnerable enough as it was, and if she allowed herself to be honest with her emotions, she was afraid she might not have the strength to tell him no.

Luckily, no such test was presented.

She awoke several hours later with the remnants of a dream fuzzy in her mind. It had to do with the drawings of Earth on the cave behind the waterfall. Suddenly, in that moment, she realized fully what she must do. She must close the bridge between Earth and Esereth. It was the only true way to save the people of Esereth from themselves. The fact that Vasin had taken some of the violent technology from Earth showed her that he would stop at nothing, no matter the cost. And it would not end with her—she was sure of it.

CHAPTER 15

A NEW BEGINNING

There is no light without love.

On the dusk of the third day of their captivity, a guard brought Sara and Daric fresh clothes, a basin of water for washing, and a tray of food.

Sara looked down at the formal dress that lay before her. It was a heavy, smooth, deep-purple fabric with a high sheen on one side.

"I'm not wearing that," Sara blurted out to the guard.

"You will. Vasin has commanded it."

She shook her head from side to side in mute protest.

In response the guard began to walk over to Sara with the likely intent to force submission.

Daric intervened. "She'll wear it. Back away." He looked at Sara with a plea of surrender in his eyes.

She acquiesced. There were too many other things that they needed to work through. It wasn't worth the fight over the clothes. The guard nodded, walked out, and closed the cell door behind him.

Neither Sara nor Daric ate more than a few bites of their food. The subtle feeling of a last supper did not motivate much of an appetite.

After the spare meal, they quickly changed clothes. There was no point in modesty. She slipped on the dress easily and looked into the small mirror on the wall. It was a contradiction—formal dress next to her grungy and disheveled appearance. She did her best with the water and washcloth to make herself presentable, but it still felt inadequate.

About thirty minutes later, the guard took both Sara and Daric from the cell. They walked up the stairs and through the castle's main corridor. Valina's palace had become so familiar to Sara in the past months that it had almost begun to feel like home. She'd also started to believe that these people meant something to her. Belief—what a powerful concept. It allowed people to do both amazing and horrible things. These people believed that she was the key to saving them, and now she believed it, too.

The guard was leading them toward the castle's inner gardens. As they entered the courtyard through the glass doors, she felt cold air on her face. Its bitterness was welcome. It let her know that she was still alive.

She saw the place was full of people—hundreds. She also could see that the entire area had been decorated. There were beautiful multicolored ribbons hanging all along the perimeter of the courtyard. Torches lined the otherwise would be dark path from the palace to the center of the garden where a recently constructed turret-shaped gazebo stood next to the great tree. With shock she realized that these decorations were for the third and final celebration.

The guards moved Daric and Sara through the crowds. They brought them both to the great tree. This was the same tree where she had found the map.

Vasin stood under the gazebo, but on a pedestal around five feet in height. He could see everyone, and they could see him. Sara's eyes were immediately drawn to what he held: Shalin in his right hand and the key in his left. Both the key and the book had a light-green glow, but neither hummed nor vibrated as Sara had seen Shalin do in the past.

Vasin spoke. "Citizens of Valina."

An immediate and abrupt hush spread over the crowd. Everyone stood waiting with a heightened sense of anticipation to see what Vasin would say and do next. The hair on the back of Sara's neck rose. This tiny physical suggestion of her fate seemed to make it all the more real.

Daric reached across at that moment to grab her hand and reassure her. He knew that she must be scared, and it was his small way of giving her some comfort. And it did give her comfort, but not for the reason he probably thought. She was not deriving discomfort from the thought of her own death, but from the selfish need to see her father, Aron, her grandmother, and even her friends back on Earth one last time. To see their faces, to give them one last hug before she left this life. She envied those who got to have family and friends around them just before death—because there was closure on both sides.

Vasin continued, "Our third and final celebration is a theme of color in light." He pointed to the decorations all around them. "It represents my promise to you of a new beginning, of rebirth. But with all new beginnings, there must be first be an ending." He pointed to the great tree and then continued, "The place where the great book was found by our ancestors will also be the place where it will be destroyed."

"So, that was the connection with the tree," she thought. It made perfect sense that she should find the map there.

Sara looked closer at some of the faces of the people of Valina as he spoke. She saw that while the anticipation was there, there was also something else— hope. What a powerful and persuasive tool.

Vasin said, "It is time. It is time to finish this and to bring back control of our own destinies."

Sara watched Vasin come down from the pedestal and step toward a large, metal-grated barrel next to the great tree. A guard leaned forward from where he stood with a torch and lit the top. It was some sort of fire pit. Sara gasped; he was going to burn the book and the key!

She lurched forward.

Daric held her back. "No, Sara, you can't!"

She watched helplessly as Vasin dropped both items into the fire.

A single tear rolled down Sara's cheek as she watched with a mixture of sorrow and desolation. It was madness, and as the firelight reflected back onto Vasin's face, it managed to further accentuate her thoughts of his insanity.

Suddenly, the air began to churn around the fire. There was a whistling sound. She watched as the fire spontaneously extinguished itself. She could see that the book and the key were pristine and unharmed, lying lifelessly in the container. Sara was astonished. She looked over at Vasin, who looked flabbergasted, too. So, fire could not harm the book and the key?

The people noticed this as well. They were confused and upset that nothing had happened. A man yelled from the crowd, "Vasin, you said this would work! You said you would save us!"

Then a group of several men started to rush toward Vasin, Daric, and Sara. The people were losing control. Today was the bubbling over of what had been seething just below the surface.

Suddenly, she saw out of the corner of her eye a Valina citizen running toward her with a knife. It was all happening so fast, and all she could do was watch with a surreal feeling of emotional detachment.

Quickly and unexpectedly, Daric jumped in front of her just in time, taking a knife wound to the chest.

This jerked her out of her fog. Sara screamed.

The attacker, a man probably in his forties, seemed to suddenly have the realization of what he had just done. He dropped the knife, wide-eyed, and backed away from Sara and Daric, disappearing into the sea-like mob of people.

She dropped onto her knees next to him on the ground. "Daric!"

He was wounded very near to his heart. It must have cut a very large artery, as a heavy amount of blood was pulsing from him as he collapsed to the ground. Daric looked up at her, eyes filled with nothing but love and admiration.

He whispered, "I love you, Sara. I would die a thousand deaths for you."

She embraced him, rocking back and forth. Blood was soaking her purple dress, turning it an almost black color. Sara could feel the tears streaming down her cheeks.

His eyes closed, and he exhaled one last long breath. It was the breath of death. It was all too quick, the wound too deep. There was no way to heal him. This was *not* how things were supposed to end.

An ordinary citizen of Valina had just murdered a man out of rage and fear. She could not allow the ones she loved—and the men, women, and children in this city—to die. Sara steadied herself, standing up from a now-lifeless Daric, and pushed through the wall of people toward the barrel where the book and key still lay.

She took a deep breath, picked up both the book and the key, and yelled as loudly as she could, "Stop! Stop all of this!"

Her voice, though scared and shaky, had a much larger impact than she would have thought possible. Almost instantaneously all the fighting and yelling ceased. Everyone looked at the trinity—the book, the key, and Sara—as she stood looking down upon them. The connections between the two universes were adjoined for the first time.

Vasin seemed to see this as well. The look on his face was one of shock.

Sara's grip tightened on both the book and the key. They were like old friends, and the bond she had formed with them was still there, now only strengthened by the reunion. But she was not the only one to feel the closeness. The book and the key began to glow and vibrate in her hands. She could also start to hear the familiar sounds from the book.

There was a sudden commotion coming from the opposite end of the garden. She could not see well that far away, but she could spot several people moving through the crowd. Her heart leaped of its own accord.

"Could it be?" she thought.

Her hands started to shake as she saw them—Aron, her father, and Aurek. Aron must have somehow found her father and told him what was happening. They had used the underground passageways to come for her.

She couldn't help the mixture of emotions. She was happy that they had come but sad, too, because this would be the last time they would be together. She saw that armed men followed them, sprouting like plants from the ground. Her father had brought reinforcements.

They rushed forward now toward the tree where Sara stood. They were all ready to fight to save her and to once and for all stop Vasin. All of her father's allies were heavily armed and ready for a final, decisive end to this fight.

Her father yelled to Vasin, who stood farther over in the crowd, in a loud, booming voice, "You are going to stop this insanity right now."

Vasin responded in a still, even voice, "Kalen, we do not agree on this, and in fact, the only thing we do agree on is that the stakes are too high not to do what we believe is right. Even if that means going into combat. We are at an impasse." He said nothing further except to nod at a heavily armed man standing a couple of feet to his left. Vasin's men advanced toward Kalen and his men.

Sara had to act immediately. She brought key toward Shalin with the intent to open it. Aron and her father ran toward her, both yelling in almost unison as they saw her action. "Sara, don't!"

Aron continued toward her, but Sara's father suddenly stopped and looked at her with a mix of agony and understanding. He knew what Sara had already figured out.

Aron shoved past handfuls of people. He reached her within seconds. They stood only a couple of inches from one another. Sara froze, though she still held the book in one hand and the key in the other. Their world had just collapsed down to the two of them.

"I can't lose you, Sara." His voice was desperate and vulnerable.

She responded to him in a whisper, "It will be all right." She leaned toward him, resting her forehead against his.

"Aron, even if I die, our planets and our universes will still be connected; just as all things are connected and always will be. Earth and Esereth are no different."

Aron responded, "And because of that truth, your death will be in vain."

But she knew that this sacrifice—her death—still meant something. "We are all destined for the same end. None of us is immortal. And so it's what we choose to do in this life, in our own moments, that sets us apart. It's what we leave behind to those who come after us that really matters. In my death, the bridge between planets will be gone, and the technologies that have killed millions will no longer be a threat to Esereth. Vasin will no longer be a threat to Esereth. And most important, the people of Esereth will believe that they have been saved and that they can make their own destiny. And it's in the power of that belief that they'll find the strength to save themselves and make their own choices."

His face still in agony, he said, "But don't you see, Sara? I can't live without you."

Sara took a deep breath and continued, "Your world still has a chance to understand what this life is really about. If Vasin and my father go to war, a true war, then your planet will have gone down the same path as Earth. You will lose your chance, and I can't allow that."

Aron suddenly shuddered at this new realization. Tears choked his words. "Sara, I love you."

She responded, "And I love you."

She felt oddly at peace. Her acceptance of her fate, and of this moment, was freeing. She wished everyone could know this tranquility. She backed away from him and raised up the book and the key. Everyone watched in astonishment as she put the key into the book. She, the book, and the key began to ascend, rising above the crowd. A bright green portal spontaneously formed directly above the great tree.

Sara knew her destination. The book and the key were becoming brighter and brighter as she moved toward the luminescent gate. They were going back to their beginning…as was she.

Suddenly, there was a blinding burst of light. The portal, Sara, the book, and the key disappeared.

EPILOGUE

The best thing about the future is
that it comes one day at a time.
—Abraham Lincoln

Sara awoke lying on the familiar floor of her bedroom at her grandmother's house. Her first thoughts were broken, discontinuous flashes of memories—Esereth—her father—Aron—Daric. Then there was a final flash that brought all of it back. She remembered everything now.

She laughed out loud suddenly. She wasn't dead! It was a surreal moment. Because she had completely accepted her death, to find out that she was still alive was, well, a bit of a mixed set of emotions. She started to wonder if perhaps it hadn't been just a crazy and vivid dream. She shook her head. "It was all too real—no way," she thought. To provide proof to this thought, she noticed that she still wore the purple dress, though stained and ripped in places. But that was nothing compared to the observation that the book and the key lay just inches away from her on the floor. She grabbed them both quickly, feeling the need to hold them close to her.

Her bedroom looked different. Most of the furniture was either missing or was covered, and at least two inches of dust layered everything. It was dark and cold in her room. What had happened here?

She jumped up and ran out the bedroom door and down the stairs.

She yelled, "Grandmother!"

No response.

The rest of the house looked just like her bedroom: empty or covered up. The whole house was, in fact, abandoned.

At the bottom of the stairs on the telephone table was a folded newspaper. It, too, had a blanket of dust on it. She picked it up and blew hard across its top, causing dust to fly everywhere. She sneezed twice because of it.

She read the header at the top of the page—the first of February 2016. Her mouth gaped open.

"This can't be right," she thought, "It's 2012."

Then she remembered…every year on Esereth was ten years on Earth.

ESERETH

VALINA

HAFU RIVER

TRAB FOREST

ANTEK

Molly Meyer-Allyn has spent her career working in the aerospace industry—from mission operations for the International Space Station (ISS) to now helping to design a human-rated commercial spacecraft. Most recently her interests have turned to writing a book about a woman's fantastic journey through life, her struggle with change, and her courage to face it all. She lives in Longmont, Colorado, with her husband and two daughters. You can learn more about her and her literary work at www.autumnonesereth.com